KU-239-615

THE GAMBLERS
OF WASTELAND

Convinced that Blackjack Chancer is behind the death of their youngest brother, Lukus and Kris Rheingold devise a plan. Lukus steals the Saturday-night takings from Chancer's casino, Wasteland Eldorado, and Kris outwits the Marshal and the Wasteland posse as they track him. The Rheingold brothers head for home, followed by the mysterious Lil Lavender, and later by Chancer and his hired gun, Fallon. All three have their reasons for hunting Lukus — and the hunt leads to a final bloody climax in the Rheingold family cemetery.

LIBRARIES NI
WITHDRAWN FROM STOCK

JIM LAWLESS

THE GAMBLERS OF WASTELAND

Complete and Unabridged

LINFORD
Leicester

First published in Great Britain in 2015 by
Robert Hale Limited
London

First Linford Edition
published 2018
by arrangement with
Robert Hale
an imprint of The Crowood Press
Wiltshire

Copyright © 2015 by Jim Lawless
All rights reserved

A catalogue record for this book is available
from the British Library.

ISBN 978–1–4448–3662–2

Published by
F. A. Thorpe (Publishing)
Anstey, Leicestershire

Set by Words & Graphics Ltd.
Anstey, Leicestershire
Printed and bound in Great Britain by
T. J. International Ltd., Padstow, Cornwall

This book is printed on acid-free paper

PART ONE

PART ONE

1

Wasteland, Texas. A ghost town one hundred miles south of the New Mexico border, on the edge of the Big Bend Desert. Home to prairie dogs and feral cats, and the occasional drifter who might unroll his blankets for a night on dry boards in a stifling room already occupied by crawling scorpions. A sun-baked wilderness of bleached timber properties invaded by termites, where coiled snakes basked on the warped boards of sagging galleries lining dusty streets and the only sounds were the creak of flimsy false fronts, the whisper of the wind and the dry rustling of rolling tumbleweed.

That was the history, the very recent reality, but the sights that met Lukus Rheingold's narrowed grey eyes as he rode in that Sunday morning were very different, though not unexpected.

Wasteland had risen from the dust when one man with money and imagination came rattling out of a town called Pine Rivers at the head of several loaded buckboards, headed south, and turned a former hotel into a gambling casino. When Lukus rode in, the Wasteland that had risen like a phoenix from the grey ashes of despair was slumbering beneath skies turned white by the fierce sun. Along both sides of the open one-hundred-yard-wide expanse of rutted ground that passed for a main street, the falling-down business premises had been regenerated by smart businessmen who had followed the money. Now selling everything from hard liquor to easy women, buildings had been hastily repaired with cheap lumber and scavenged six-inch nails; they sported new, high false fronts on which names had been crudely splashed in black paint: *Guns. Feed. General Store. Mick's Irish Saloon.*

The building Lukus Rheingold was

looking for stood out from its neighbours. Wasteland Eldorado. A much bigger two-storey structure, the former hotel had been coated with brighter paint and made more outrageous promises. *Keno, Chuck-a-luck, Poker, Craps, Roulette. Proprietor Blackjack Chancer. Step inside once, folks, step out set up for life.* In the past six months ranchers, cowboys, drifters and hoboes had walked through the doors sharing a dream. Most had walked out a few short hours later with the lining hanging out of their pants' pockets.

One of those men, Lukus thought with silent, controlled fury, went into that glittering emporium penniless but full of youthful hope. Hours later he was carried out, a sagging, lifeless, blood-soaked figure, and tossed unceremoniously on to the undertaker's black-painted buggy.

Christian Rheingold, the youngest of the three Rheingold brothers, now a month dead.

A mangy cat strutted disdainfully in

front of Lukus's horse. The roan faltered nervously, began back-stepping as the cat moved away towards the plank walk and a tumbleweed came skittering before a hot gust of wind. Then, in answer to a flick of the reins, the horse carried its rider across to the hitch rail in front of Wasteland Eldorado.

Lukus swung down, keeping a loose grip on the reins. He was a tall man, lean and muscular, his height masked by the breadth of his powerful shoulders. Though he was closing in on his thirtieth year, anyone pinned like a moth by the sharp gaze of his grey eyes would figure him for an older man, a wiser man, and certainly one it would be dangerous to cross. For the wisdom they recognized was the life-preserving kind that comes of necessity to a man with long experience of riding on the wrong side of the law. Lukus Rheingold had left home young, built himself a reputation with fists and gun and become infamous throughout the West under an assumed name. He had returned to the family spread on the Rio Grande only when word came that both his parents had died.

For a moment, making good use of that hard-earned wisdom, Lukus rested his elbows on the saddle and let his eyes rove the length of the gambling emporium's gallery. The old hotel's garish façade featured a number of upper windows where grubby net curtains hung to either side of dusty glass. Living quarters, Lukus thought. All the action takes place on the ground floor. And suddenly, with a vivid image in his mind of the violent direction which that action was about to take, he was a happy man. There was a young life to be avenged. He and his brother had devised a plan. The intention was to ride away with a gunny-sack filled with Blackjack Chancer's cash, and leave a clear message that it was payment for the murder committed in his Eldorado. It was a good plan, but of no use whatsoever if it all went wrong here in Wasteland.

So Lukus let his gaze range further afield. Through eyes narrowed against the dazzling sun he confirmed the convenient location of the jail, a stone building a good hundred yards away on the far side of the ridiculously wide thoroughfare. That made it far enough away for the Wasteland marshal to be unaware of any trouble until Lukus was ready to let him know — and letting the marshal know, letting him get a good glimpse of Lukus Rheingold as he rode away like a bat out of hell, was all an essential part of the plan.

But first, his target was the office that was almost certainly situated behind the Eldorado's main gambling room. On any Sunday morning Blackjack Chancer was sure to be in there, eyes hooded as he licked his fingers and counted the dirty banknotes that were the Saturday-night takings.

Takings that Kris, Lukus's remaining, younger brother, had on several nights watched being wagered on cards, dice and spinning balls, only to swept away across the gambling tables and scooped up by blank-eyed croupiers or red-lipped girls with golden hair and false smiles.

Kris had grown a straggly beard, disguised the cruel limp caused by his game leg as best he could, and played the part of a bumbling country boy who didn't know a black ace from a red deuce. Head bent, always ensuring he was lost amongst the rabble of excited gamblers, his sharp eyes had never been still. From what he had seen he was able to report back to Lukus that losing just one Saturday night's takings would hurt Chancer badly; his warning had been that in that Eldorado gambling room there were armed men who would ensure that a bold thief would never make it out of the door.

But that was on Saturday nights. Lukus surmised that while totting up those takings on a Sunday morning, Chancer would have just one man in the office with him, riding shotgun. He'd be a man with the lean and hungry look of a prowling wolf, a man with watchful eyes, a double-barrelled scattergun propped against the desk and a hand never straying more than a quick stab away from a well-used six-gun. But even a wolf can become careless. For that man, today would be just another in a long succession of Sunday mornings. And on Sunday mornings in Blackjack Chancer's back office, trouble was something that never reared its ugly head, and the only disturbing sound would be when the gambling magnate took a fresh lick at his fingers.

With a chill smile that would have frightened the life out of the haughty cat, Lukus Rheingold took a canvas sack out of one of his saddle-bags. He settled his gunbelt, tugged the brim of his dusty Stetson down low on his forehead. Then, leading the big roan, he set off around the side of the building. As he did so a buckboard pulled by a glistening chestnut mare dragged a trail of fine dust down the length of the wide street. The driver was dressed in black, and wore a top hat. Lukus thought he saw the sunlight catch the man's eyes as he glanced across towards the Chancer premises. The wagon trundled on for fifty yards or so, then came to a halt alongside one of the business establishments.

Undertaker. *Someone's cashed in his chips*, Lukus thought briefly, then banished the man from his mind.

Cautious now, he led the horse around to the rear of the building. The sun was not yet high, and the rear walls were in shade. He kept his hand close to the roan's muzzle, ready to stifle any sudden snort or whinny. He walked close to the unpainted timber; reached the door; stopped; listened.

Not a sound from inside. Old timber was crackling in the heat of the sun. There was the faint sound of distant laughter, and for an instant Lukus was distracted as he imagined the undertaker he had seen cracking an irreverent joke.

Then he dropped the horse's reins, left them trailing on the hard earth. Taking a deep breath, Lukus swung away, lunged forward to kick open the door and burst into the building with drawn six-gun.

A huge oak table took up most of the centre of the room. On it were worn, leather-bound ledgers, bundles of banknotes and scatterings of silver dollars — gold eagles and double eagles. Almost buried by the piles of banknotes there was a six-gun with a fancy bone butt and engraved barrel. A big muscular man with a flowing mane of straw-coloured hair turning to grey was standing by an open safe. A black string tie emphasized the white of his shirt. Gold rings glittered on his fingers. As he swung to face the intruder, keen blue eyes with a hint of cruelty stared at Lukus without apparent emotion. That it was there, carefully masked, was revealed to Lukus by the man's instinctive glance towards his six-gun — several steps out of his reach.

Then an inner door on the far side of the room swung open and a man stepped into the office. The man riding shotgun. A man with empty eyes, sallow, swarthy skin that suggested mixed blood, and a thin half-smile. Tall, whipcord-thin, black clothing, black flat-crowned hat, he wore a low-slung holster with a well-used six-gun hanging from a gunbelt packed with shiny brass shells.

'Morning, gents,' Lukus said.

The big man eased away from the safe, looked with open disdain at Lukus's levelled pistol.

'Who the hell are you?'

'I'm the man who's about to clean out your safe. You're Blackjack Chancer. Introductions over.'

Lukus tossed the canvas sack carelessly on to the cluttered desk. Coins slid clinking across the scarred woodwork and fell in glittering metallic showers to the hard floor where they rolled like fleeing cockroaches. Banknotes drifted like falling leaves.

13

'Fill it,' Lukus said.

'Like hell,' the big man said casually, and he looked across at the lean man with the empty eyes. 'You going to stand there? I pay you to overcome minor irritations like this — right? Like swatting flies, I'd say. So get to it.'

The gunman was looking hard at Lukus Rheingold.

He said, 'Don't I know you, feller?'

'Can't recall our paths crossing,' Lukus said, 'though I sure as hell know the breed, if not the individual.'

'That's not what I said. But if I'm right, the name you've given here is all wrong.'

'And you're wasting time. Walk over there, help the reluctant Mister Chancer to fill that sack.'

The lean gunman nodded slowly, his empty eyes never leaving Lukus. Like a dancer, he took a sideways step towards Chancer as if to comply. Then, a snake striking, he turned, bent at the knees and went for his gun.

His arm was fast, registering as a

blur. But, fast as he moved, he was no match for a man who had the drop. Lukus allowed the gunman the luxury of clamping his hand on the worn butt. Saw not a glimmer of emotion in the blank eyes, though the gunman must have known he was staring death in the face. Leather rasped. The gun cleared the holster. Cold metal flashed in the sunlight slanting through the window.

Lukus coolly shot him in the upper arm. He saw the sleeve rip. The instant bloody gash in flesh. The six-gun fell to the floor. The gunman clamped his hand to his arm. Blood leaked through his fingers. His lips had tightened, but he uttered no sound, and the eyes were unchanged.

A sound dragged Lukus's eyes to Chancer. The gambler had his hand on the safe's door and was about to slam it shut. If he managed that, and spun the wheel, the game was lost.

'Leave it.'

Lukus snapped the command, backed it with the six-gun. He aimed the smoking muzzle at the centre of the big man's face, knowing the type: a vain man, Chancer would worry about his handsome countenance, with the thought of death coming a poor second.

The gambling man cursed softly, dropped his hand from the door. But he couldn't prevent his eyes flicking towards the gunman. Again Lukus sensed movement. When he swung to face the threat, the lean man was down on the floor and had already swept the fallen six-gun into his left hand.

With a grunt of effort Lukus grabbed the edge of the heavy oak table and heaved it over. Money showered down on the wounded gunman. The table came to rest on its side. The edge of its top clamped the gunman's legs to the dirt floor.

Again Lukus turned the six-gun's muzzle on Blackjack Chancer.

'Do like I say and fill the sack,' he said, 'or I'll put a bullet through one knee, then the other, then both your elbows. But I don't want to do that. That shot will have been heard, which means I'm short of time. Give me banknotes, no coins. And don't get choosy. I'll take all denominations from a dollar bill all the way up to the biggest you've got.'

Chancer's face had turned a pasty white beneath its tan, but it was from anger, not fear. Without a word the Eldorado's owner swept the sack off the desk. He rolled back his chair, took three strides to the safe and began filling the sack. He was still rock steady. His square hands showed no sign of a tremor. Watching him, Lukus was listening only absently to the rustle of banknotes, the creaks from the table as the gunman hidden by its bulk struggled to free himself.

Wasteland's marshal was a man called Crane. He'd served his apprenticeship as a lawman in the wild cow towns of Kansas. What Lukus was listening for were noises from the street that would tell him the lawman had heard the shot, had fixed the location and was moving in fast.

Lukus wanted that, but not yet, not now. He wanted the marshal to come after him, but at a time of his choosing. And that time would be when he was on his horse and heading out of town.

Chancer was taking his time.

'Hurry it up,' Lukus snapped.

The gunman had struggled out from under the table. He'd made it to his feet, but his face glistened with the cold sweat of pain. And he'd lost his six-gun. Like Chancer's pistol with its fancy grips, it lay somewhere under the scattered banknotes.

'Relax, we're almost done here,' Lukus said. He grinned at the gunman and waggled his six-gun.

'I know you,' the man said. His voice was a whisper. His sleeve was soaked in blood. 'From somewhere, I know you, and it'll come to me. Then we'll see.'

'When it does come to you,' Lukus said, 'I'll be long gone.'

Chancer turned from the safe. He

fixed Lukus with a gaze in which amusement lurked. Then he flung the heavy sack towards him in a looping arc. Lukus turned sideways, taking the weight with his left hip. Then, carefully, ensuring that his six-gun was covering the big gambling man, he bent at the knees and picked up the sack with his left hand.

'Nice try,' he said, 'but a word of warning. You've lost some cash. You'll make that up, and more, from the suckers who play your tables in the next few days. But make a wrong move now and it's your life you'll lose.'

Dragging the sack, he backed towards the door. He was watched pensively by the wounded gunman, with amused aplomb by Blackjack Chancer.

'If you walk out the door with that money,' the gambling tycoon said, 'you're as good as dead. You'll be found. When you are, you'll pay in blood and pain. There's no distance too great, no hiding-place good enough . . . '

He was still mouthing threats when Lukus backed swiftly out of the door, dragged it shut by its broken lock and ran to the roan. He flung himself into the saddle. The sack was in his left hand, its rich weight destroying his balance. In his right hand he held his six-gun. He planted the heavy sack between his thighs. Scooping up the reins he backed the horse, fired three fast shots that drilled holes in the door's timber. Then he spun the horse and clattered away from the building.

He walked the horse on to the wide expanse of the town's main street. Once there, he turned to look towards the jail. The stone building, on the other side of the hundred-yard expanse of street, at the end of the block of mismatched timber buildings, showed no signs of life.

The single shot that he had fired in Chancer's office, the three fired when he was leaving, had not been heard.

Deliberately, Lukus cocked his pistol and fired off the remaining shots into the hot, still air. Waited. Watched. He was rewarded. A tall figure emerged from the stone building. Stood with hands on hips, staring up the street. Swiftly, Lukus reloaded. He fired six shots at the distant figure, saw each bullet kick up the dry dust of the street. Then he turned the roan and took it up the street at a steady trot. The hot sun was burning on his shoulders. The dust kicked up by his horse's hoofs was acrid, choking.

Lukus counted mentally to fifty. Then he flung a swift glance over his shoulder.

The man who had emerged from the jail was running up the street. A badge glittered on his vest. He was watched by the undertaker, who had rushed out of his premises at the shooting and was standing by the buckboard. And now Blackjack Chancer was there, out in front of his Eldorado. He was watching Lukus, at the same time gesturing wildly to the approaching lawman.

When Lukus faced front again and

spurred the roan into a gallop, his eyes were bright with exultation. The first stage of the audacious scheme to make Blackjack Chancer pay for his sins had gone without mishap. The proof lay in the heavy sack of stolen money draped across the saddle horn and the image of the Wasteland gambling man as he stood fuming outside his Eldorado, angrily flapping his arms like a flustered hen at the advancing town marshal.

The second stage would involve both those men and require some time to set up. The encounter with the gambler and the law would inevitably carry risks, and be fraught with danger. But, just as Lukus Rheingold's strength had seen the first encounter go according to plan, in the second stage it would be another man's weakness that would make men blind to the obvious and help carry the day.

2

They rode steadily out of Wasteland, a five-man posse headed by town marshal Jed Crane. The riders were led by a 'breed called Zac on a ragged paint pony who rode fifty yards ahead of the main bunch. He was twisted loosely in the saddle, one hand on the horn, his eyes cast down on the clear tracks in the dust. An unnecessary use of age-old skills, in Crane's opinion. If the fugitive stuck to the trail only a fool would need an Indian to point out the obvious.

Buck Aitken was Crane's deputy, a laconic six-footer who had been in partnership with the big lawman from beginnings in Tombstone, Arizona, then through several years taming wild, drunken cowpokes in the cow towns of southern Kansas. Grey-haired Tom Duncan was Wasteland's gunsmith, and had answered Crane's call because

Sundays were dead days and he craved excitement.

The fifth man was Blackjack Chancer. He rode a magnificent palomino, but had thrown himself angrily into the saddle without changing his Sunday-morning office attire. The only addition was a dove-grey Stetson, and a gunbelt and holster from which jutted the bone butt of the engraved Colt .45 he'd hastily scrambled to recover from among the fallen banknotes. His long hair brushed the collar of the white shirt. His gaze was stormy as he looked across at Crane.

'That sonofabitch took enough off my table and out of the safe to pay you and your deputy's wages for a year or more,' he said. 'I want it back, every last dollar, and I want his head on a platter.'

'We'll do our best,' Crane said, amused. 'He rode fast, which is always the way when a man's trying to outpace fear, but a horse can keep that up only for so long.'

'Then we'll catch him. And when we

do he'll rue the day he crossed my path.'

Five miles out of Wasteland, the posse riding in a roughly northerly direction, the trail was joined by another, snaking around a stand of trees as it came in from the east. At that fork the 'breed pulled his paint to a halt. When the others joined him he pointed to tracks.

'Buckboard,' he said. 'Came out of there not too long ago, can't be too far ahead.'

Crane shrugged. 'Nothing to do with us.'

'Who can say?' the Indian said with the easy patience of his kind, and again he pushed on ahead.

A couple of miles further on the five men brought their horses around a rocky bluff. Where a sparse scattering of cottonwoods lined the fast-flowing waters of No End Creek, the hot sun beat down on a scene of chaos. A buckboard was lying tilted into the water. One of the back wheels had slipped down the soft grassy bank and into the creek. To Crane, edging his horse along close to the water as he rode in, it looked as if the wheel had dropped from the bank and hit sloping flat stones that were under water and slick with moss. It had then slithered sideways under the buckboard's weight and dropped deeper into the water.

'Mule up front, horse on a trail rope — and damn me if there ain't a coffin tied on the flatbed.'

Aitken had it right. The coffin, Crane saw, had snapped tight the ropes holding it when the wagon slid into the creek and was now up against the side boards. The mule in the traces had its ears flattened, probably figuring it should do something but defeated by the wagon's weight. Behind the buckboard the horse on a tie-rope was snorting its unease and straining backwards, eyes rolling.

Then the posse was up with the wagon. They pulled their mounts to a halt, the drifting dust dun-coloured in the hot sunlight. As they formed a loose half-circle around the stranded buckboard a young man appeared. Up to his thighs in the icy waters on the creek side of the wagon, he hefted a dripping saddle up over the side boards and dumped it alongside the coffin. Then, limping badly, he splashed up on to the bank, said something softly to the skittish horse, and looked expectantly at Crane.

'Jed Crane, Wasteland marshal,' Crane said. 'Looks like you've got trouble here.'

The young man nodded. 'Joe Martin,' he said. 'You just missed the action. The wheel slipped over the edge. No real damage except to my pride.'

'That could be me talking. There's been a robbery in Wasteland. One man. He walked into a gambling joint bold as brass. He left town rich, and in one hell of a hurry. Headed this way. You see him?'

'Nobody,' Martin said. He was

watching the Indian. He'd detached himself from the group and kneed his pony away up the trail. He held his mount to a walk as he leaned out of the saddle, this time serious in his work, sharp eyes backed by wisdom closely studying the ground.

'Zac there' — Crane jerked his chin at the 'breed — 'reckons you came out of the fork a couple of miles back.'

'My kid brother was busting broncs on the Lazy B. Came off a real mean stallion, broke his neck.' Martin nodded at the coffin. 'Ma insists he's buried with his grandparents behind the family spread, so I'm taking him home.'

Blackjack Chancer was seething.

'How long ago d'you say this happened?' He rode his horse in close, glowering at the dripping young man.

Martin spread his hands. 'Ten, fifteen minutes.'

'So you came out of that fork maybe a half-hour ago,' Chancer said. 'That damned thief *must* have rode past you.'

'I told you, I've seen nobody.'

'What about we ask Zac?' Chancer said, turning on Crane. 'If he's a tracker worth his salt he'll know if the thief went past before the buckboard came out the fork.'

'Maybe,' Crane said. 'But I can't see how it helps if this kid did see him. If the man who stole your money did go past the buckboard, he's ahead of us and we're wasting time.'

Then the Indian came back down the trail. He looked at Crane, his face impassive.

'Rode a fast couple of hundred yards, slowed, then straight into the creek. I ride a mile, maybe I see where he come out again.'

'Or maybe not,' Tom Duncan said. 'He could've come out this bank further up the trail, or rode across and up the other side of the creek. By now he could be in the next county.'

The Indian was stoic. He said, 'It's an old trick. Use a fast-running creek to hide tracks. In time I'd pick up the trail.'

'We ain't got time,' Jed Crane said. He saw the 'breed sniffing, cocked his head. 'What you got?'

'That.' The 'breed jerked his head at the coffin. 'Something in there is ripe. Hell, you got a blocked nose you can't smell it?'

Crane eased his horse closer, leaned across into the wagon, pulled back with a grimace.

Martin's face was blank. 'He's been dead a while,' he said, 'and where he was on the Lazy B there was no undertaker within a couple of days' ride.'

'One in Wasteland,' Crane said, watching Martin. 'I know of the Lazy B. Half a day's ride from town, maybe less.'

'I guess the folks I worked for bury their own dead.' Martin shrugged. 'The foreman got word to me fast as he could, but it took time for me to get here.'

Crane was waiting. When nothing more was forthcoming, he said, 'Get

30

here from where?'

'Rio Grande. Just a small spread. Pa never did give it a name.'

Crane nodded, as if not entirely satisfied but in a hurry. He jerked a thumb at the buckboard. 'That's sure wedged some. With just the one mule, you'll need help dragging it out of the creek.'

'Tip the coffin in the creek, lighten the load,' Blackjack Chancer said cruelly. 'A watery grave for your brother's as good as any, and you'll have got rid of that stink.'

Martin shook his head. 'I'll manage, use the horse if necessary,' he said. For some reason he looked amused.

Still unsure, Crane gave the young man a searching glance.

'I noticed you limping when you came out of the water. You know what they say about pride coming before a fall. There's no shame in a man who's injured himself calling for some extra muscle.'

'The injury came before I was born,'

Martin said, 'so it's something I've grown with, and learned to work with or around.'

Crane gave a brief nod of acknowledgement. Then, touching a gloved hand to his hat brim, he spurred off up the trail with the other members of the small posse hot on his heels.

*   *   *

Martin watched the posse hammer away up the trail, pass the point where the 'breed said the thief's tracks had entered the creek, head on up the slope beyond the trees and out into the bright sunlight, to be lost in the dust and the heat haze. He waited, leaning against the buckboard, rolled a cigarette. Then he eased off his boots and emptied out the creek water, put them on again and pulled a face at the wet and the cold of his saturated socks.

After five minutes his feet were warmer. Again he looked up the trail. The dust had settled. The sound of hoofs had long faded into silence. The haze hid nothing but emptiness. Somewhere a bird was singing. Insects hummed lazily. He flicked the cigarette into the creek. Then he put two fingers to his mouth and gave a shrill whistle. The mule jumped, startled, swung its head to stare. The horse backed off, again snapping the trail rope taut.

Then a rider came out of the thick stands of trees on No End Creek's opposite bank. He spurred his horse down the steep slope into the water and splashed across to surge up the bank close to the buckboard.

'Everything went OK then, Mr Martin?' he said, dismounting with a broad grin.

'You heard that?'

'I moved to the edge of the trees 'case there was trouble.'

Kris Rheingold laughed. 'Martin was the first name that came to my head.'

'Could have been a slip,' Lukus Rheingold said. 'If you recall, that's the name of the Wasteland undertaker. But nobody noticed.'

'So now we finish off,' Kris said.

'Yes indeed. They'll listen to the Indian, he'll find nothing so they'll be back before too long. We go ahead as planned. Their first surprise will be finding the buckboard where they left it.'

'And the second will be in the coffin and knock them sideways,' Kris Rheingold said, and with a wink at his brother he climbed on to the wagon and began unscrewing the coffin's lid.

★ ★ ★

It was late afternoon when Jed Crane brought the small posse straggling back down the trail. The man immediately behind him was Buck Aitken. They'd wasted a considerable amount of time, and from the outset Crane's deputy had been dead set against what he'd reckoned was a pointless chase.

Now Crane heard Aitken grunt, then spit his anger towards the creek: he'd caught sight of the buckboard, its warped boards painted by the last rays of the setting sun. Still canted into the rushing waters, it was deserted.

'Maybe we should swap badges,' Crane offered, pulling his sorrel back to a walk. 'You weigh up situations better than me, seem to have got it right again.'

He turned with a wry grin as Aitken chuckled.

Then grey-haired Tom Duncan swept by at a gallop, closely followed by the Indian, Zac, and Blackjack Chancer. The three bore down on the buck-board, pulled their horses to a halt in a cloud of dust.

Aitken was shaking his head. 'Hell, I know Chancer must be raging but there's no call now for all that haste,' he said. 'What's the sayin', no point shutting the stable door when the horse has bolted?'

'Or mule,' Crane said. 'I see Mr Martin took that with him when he lit out.'

'Yeah, and that's just what I would do if I had a load to carry.'

'We can't be sure what we see here's connected to the robbery. If that story about the Lazy B was right, Martin was nowhere near Wasteland.'

'But the feller we were hunting rode on by that buckboard and chose a spot to drop into the creek,' Aitken said. 'That sent us chasing miles up the trail. Who's to say he didn't drop into the creek and simply make his way back to the buckboard.'

'Be a neat trick.' Crane squinted at Aitken. 'You talking about the coffin? Are you saying that's where the sack of stolen money was hidden, under our noses?'

Aitken grinned. 'Good choice of words, as I recall.'

'That Martin, he said it was his kid brother in there,' Crane said absently, but he was watching the three up ahead.

Zac was up on the buckboard, standing braced over the coffin. As

Crane and Aitken pulled alongside the wagon and swung down, Tom Duncan turned away. He was grimacing and pressing a bandanna to his face. Chancer had swung his palomino away, and was staring broodingly into the distance.

'Zac?' Crane called.

'You'll want to see this,' Zac said. 'If this is their kid brother, he must be one of them wolves likes wearing sheep's clothes.'

The wagon rocked when Crane pulled himself aboard. His weight caused a wheel to slip off a stone, the wagon to slide further into the creek. Crane lurched unsteadily, grabbed hold of the Indian's arm, peered over his shoulder. The coffin's lid had been unscrewed. It was leaning lengthwise against the open box.

'Holy cow,' he said softly, and Zac chuckled.

'Alive or dead, that is no cow, my friend.'

Crane jerked upright, holding a hand

to his mouth. The crude wooden box was almost wholly occupied by the suppurating carcass of a sheep. The stink of putrefaction was sweet and sickening. Crane, disgusted, swung hastily away.

'You see what I see?' Zac said.

'Sure,' Crane said thickly. 'And we both know what that means.'

He jumped down, dragged the back of his hand across his wet mouth, sucked in a deep and ragged breath.

Aitken was watching him.

'What is it? I got it worked out that stink comes from a dead sheep, but what did Zac mean?'

'You hit the nail on the head, Buck. Martin left a couple of fifty-dollar bills stuck to the carcass in case we were too stupid to figure things out. He also used a stone out of the creek as a weight to hold down a newspaper cutting. It's a bloody mess, smeared to hell and back, but even a glance was enough for me to know why the robber went after Chancer.'

'Lost a heap of cash gambling,

recouping his losses?' Then Aitken shook his head. 'No, that wouldn't get in the newspapers.'

'This bit of news came out a month ago, written by a Houston journalist. All about a kid died a violent death in a gambling joint in Wasteland owned by a certain Blackjack Chancer.'

He raised his voice on the last few words. Chancer, who'd ridden off in frustration, swung the palomino and kneed it over to Crane.

'What did you say?'

'You heard me,' Crane said bluntly. 'There's a torn scrap of newsprint in that coffin ties the robbery to the kid who breathed his last over one of your craps tables. I wanted you locked up for that, but too many of the witnesses were on your payroll. Well, it looks like this was the boy's kinfolk getting back at you for that bloody killing. So, as of now, me and my deputy're washing our hands of the whole affair. You want your money back, Chancer, go after the thief yourself.'

PART TWO

PART TWO

3

One week later a hard-faced woman on a chestnut mare emerged from tall aspens cloaking a gentle slope and pushed on down through the long grass with a pat on the neck and a soft murmur of approval for the horse. She had spotted the small ranch house and its outbuildings and corral from the ridge. It was at the end of a winding, rutted trail that she knew led to the west Texas town of Nathan's Ford. A mile or so beyond the property she had been seeking, the Rio Grande was a ribbon of molten steel in the afternoon sunlight. On its near bank stood another ranch, a sprawl of house, barns and corrals. The drab, dun-coloured landscape of Mexico stretched from the river's western banks away into the distant heat haze.

As she neared the bottom of the

slope she could hear the regular thunk, thunk of an axe. She took the mare across the trail, nodding understanding and satisfaction as the horse picked its way daintily over the deep ruts. Well-used ruts, the woman noted, on either side of undisturbed grass. The trail had seen frequent use by a wagon — a buckboard if she had it right. And from the ridge her searching gaze had told her that there was no wagon of any kind at this spread: just one horse and a mule lazily swishing their tails in the corral.

Everything added up. But two men should mean two horses. Where was the second man?

The noise of the axe came as no surprise, because from a distance she had seen the man splitting logs. From the knowledge she had gained in Wasteland, from what she had witnessed there, she was almost certain that the man wielding the axe was not Lukus Rheingold.

Then, almost as if the horse had

taken her there of its own volition, she was round the house and moving between the corral and the rear of the building to where the man was working.

'Good afternoon,' she said, drawing rein. She'd composed her features, wiping away the hard look, tried softening her gaze but without much success. The eyes were the window to the soul, she thought, and knowing what lurked there she allowed the shadow of a smile to curve her lips.

He was stripped to the waist. The sight of the woman on horseback caused him some embarrassment. He cast a glance to where his shirt had been tossed carelessly on the growing pile of split logs, took a half-step towards it; she immediately noticed how he favoured his right leg. Then he seemed to realize that grabbing his shirt would merely draw attention to his nakedness. He planted the axe head on the hard earth at his feet, folded his hands on the end of the axe's long handle and flashed a brilliant smile.

'Afternoon, ma'am.'

'Is Lukus around?'

If he was surprised at her use of the name, he didn't show it. 'I saw you come over the ridge,' he said. 'Watched you all the way down. From way up there you could surely see the house, make up your own mind.'

'Of course. Lukus rides a fine roan, and there's just your horse and an old mule in the corral.'

'Are you telling me, or asking?'

'Neither asking nor telling, but looking for the right response.'

'Are you always this cagey?'

'Not cagey. It's been a long, hard ride, Kris, and I want to talk to Lukus.'

He said nothing, again registering no surprise when a woman he had never seen before used his name.

She nodded slowly, her eyes roving beyond the pile of split logs. 'Two brothers, and a small graveyard in those trees over there. I'm old enough to have seen enough tragedy to draw the right conclusions. Also, there's no livestock, no crops. This hasn't been a working spread for some time.'

'I'm working.'

'Not much money in logs. But you don't look like you starve, so you must get money — one way or another.' She paused there, and looked at him as if again waiting for a response. When none came, she said, 'Lukus is in town.'

'Again, you're telling, not asking.'

'Thinking aloud.'

'Yes, Lukus is in town,' Kris Rheingold said.

'Thank you.' Her gaze was shrewd. 'I'm sure you know what this is about, but out of respect I'm going first to the older brother.'

'Elder.'

She bit her lower lip, raised an eyebrow.

'Well now . . . '

She touched the mare lightly, backed it on to a patch of rough grass, turned to go.

'Like it or not, you're going to see me again,' she called; then she was gone, this time not crossing the trail but riding alongside it on the softer ground as she pushed on towards the town.

★ ★ ★

High up on the ridge, the two men watched the horse and rider until they disappeared beyond the stands of trees flanking the trail into town and the sound of hoofbeats, softened by the lush grass, had faded into silence.

Blackjack Chancer cleared his throat, looked down the slope speculatively as the man standing in front of the house kept his eyes on the receding rider for a little longer than was necessary before returning to the yard and attacking the logs.

'Right place — or not?' the big man said.

The other man, the tall, thin gunslinger who called himself Fallon and wore black clothing and a black, flat-crowned hat, shrugged wide shoulders. 'There's only one way to find out.'

'She led us this far, seemed to know what she was doing. No deviation. Clear across the Big Bend Desert. Stopped a couple of times at water holes.'

'If this is the Rheingold place, she's been working for you and doesn't know it.'

'Rheingold,' Chancer mused. 'You never did tell me how you dug up that name.'

'Marshal Jed Crane. Undertaker told him, he told me. Couldn't or wouldn't tell me where to find 'em, but it seems Lil's led you to them and your cash. But what's in it for her?'

'She's a woman who had it all and lost everything in one hot afternoon. Her kind never forgets. She's been watching me for six months, settin' on that damn rooming-house gallery with those fancy op'ry glasses pinned to her cold blue eyes.'

'Been watching each other, you and her,' Fallon said.

'Sure. And then she made a move. A

week after my money went, she walked down the Wasteland livery, told Davy to get her horse ready for a long ride. Which brings us up to date. When she left we were eating her dust. We're here. She's here. And we both know: with my money she could start up again — if that's what she's after.' Chancer grinned. 'Whatever it is she's after, it's a damn shame she's ridden all this way for nothing.'

'One man down there,' Fallon said, still watching the house. 'A Rheingold if she's got it right, but not the man as stole your cash and cut a groove in my arm.'

'His brother. I got that from Crane; there were three brothers, now there's two.'

'Well now,' Fallon said softly.

Chancer shot him a glance. 'You've got a smouldering temper there, Fallon, could be your downfall.'

'A lot of men have brothers,' Fallon mused. 'You ever hear the story of Achilles and his heel?'

'If you're thinking of using the brother to get at the man who had the drop on you and made it count — '

'What we're both thinking of is your money, so we go down, ask polite questions.'

'That was my thought,' Chancer said, 'but we'll give it a while before moving in. Let that feller tire himself, let his muscles cry out for relief.' The big man smiled. 'We both know polite questions won't do it, so this way you're making it easy for yourself, Fallon. Who knows, maybe in the end we'll both get what we're after.'

'With those two losers, both of us with a grudge and you with that temper you never could control?' Fallon's chuckle was cruel. 'It was never going to be all that difficult, was it, now?' the tall man said. He settled himself in the saddle and began to build a cigarette.

4

When Lukus Rheingold checked the time on Will Travis's polished longcase clock as he left the lawyer's office, it was four in the afternoon. For a brief moment he thought maybe it was time he collected his horse from Bud Jennings's livery barn and headed home. Then a faint, ironic grin lightened his sombre expression.

He and Kris had spent a leisurely morning — as rich folks do. When Lukus left for Nathan's Ford just after noon, his brother had been wielding an axe, splitting logs into kindling and firewood ready for the long winter months. He'd finish that task, Lukus thought, use cold water and strong soap to wash the sweat of honest toil from hot skin and aching muscles, then relax out front in the sun with a satisfied sigh and a long cool drink.

The last thing he'd want was his elder brother yapping on yet again about the pile of money they'd acquired dishonestly, unlawfully and at great risk, only to discover it was more trouble than it was worth.

And yet, Lukus brooded, what the hell was there to keep him in town? He'd passed the time of day with a couple of men he'd come to know well, bought some shells and tobacco which he'd taken to the barn and stuffed into his saddle-bags, then crossed the street and had a couple of glasses of warm beer in Alan Spence's Wayfarer saloon.

There he had spent a few minutes chatting with his nearest neighbours, a man called Cage and his ranching partner, Violet Goodwine. Goodwine was a former owner of the Wayfarer. A couple of years back she had got involved with Cage in a series of bloody gunfights across the river in Mexico. Back on Texas soil, there had been a terrifying showdown during which Cage had saved Goodwine's life — with a little help from Alan Spence. The end result had been Goodwine's selling the Wayfarer to Spence. She and Cage set up in partnership on Cage's inherited ranch. Renamed the V Slash C, it was located between the much smaller Rheingold spread and the Rio Grande.

From the saloon, Lukus had made a point of dropping in on lawyer Will Travis. Which, of course, had been a complete waste of time.

Lukus and the lawyer had become friends when Lukus, returning after those long years away from the family fold, had called in to discuss the financial standing of the Rheingold holding. Will, a tall, gangling man with a face like rich, lined leather, had deep-set grey eyes that always appeared to be looking into the far distance.

By his looks, Travis would have been more at home out in the high timber with a hunting rifle in the crook of his arm and a faithful hound-dog at heel. The truth was that at times he'd confessed to Lukus that he yearned after that life. Nevertheless, at his desk he remained, out of place but dedicated, a square peg in a round hole with a mind as sharp as a razor and always with a wry smile twitching the moustache as he dealt with legal matters.

Lukus's problem had been that he couldn't figure out how to tell a respectable attorney-at-law — and friend — that he and his brother had stolen a fortune in banknotes, at gunpoint, and now didn't know what to do with it. That, wrapped in a tarpaulin and safely hidden, there lay a heap of money belonging to a gambling man from Wasteland, Texas. How do you ask that friend what you should do when you know you can't deposit it in a bank for fear of raising suspicion, can't spend it in great chunks for the same damn reason and don't want to set fire to it because, while that would a final solution, it would mean the risks taken had all been for nothing?

The answer is, you don't.

Because like as not Will Travis would

take one look at your honest countenance and either commit you to the
nearest establishment for folks who've
lost their marbles, or march you down
to the marshal's office and see you
locked into the nearest strap-steel cell.

Neither of those options appealed to
Lukus. He was having a hard enough
time adjusting to life on the straight and
narrow after years when, hunter or
hunted, he was constantly drunk on
wild rushes of adrenaline. He had been
back six months when boredom set in.
It had been followed by restlessness he
found difficult to resist. While the
killing of his younger brother had been
a tragedy — hell, in those six months
he'd barely got to know the young man
he'd last seen as an infant — the
turbulent aftermath which terminated
in the Wasteland robbery had once
again got the adrenaline juices flowing.

But that had been a week ago. So,
now what? One long day was the same
as the last, the next unlikely to be any
different. Restlessness was a siren call

urging him to hit the trail — but how could he ride away from Kris, a young man born with a crippled right leg, who idolized his remaining brother? Again the answer was easy: he couldn't. And Lukus was standing irresolutely on the edge of the plank walk in the fading afternoon sunlight, wondering what the hell to do with his life while breathing in the cool air wafting in from the Rio Grande, when the woman crept up behind him. She spoke one short sentence, the suddenness and the import of which caused him to jump out of his skin.

'Dammit,' he blurted, 'you scared me half to death.' Then he took one look at her and, spilling a jumble of words, apologized profusely for his language.

She was almost tall enough to meet his gaze on the level, strong-boned and slim, fifty going on sixty. Her thick, blonde-grey hair was worn long and snatched back from her angular face in a ponytail. She was clad in a worn leather vest over a dove-grey shirt, a dark, split riding-skirt that brushed the tops of her ankle boots. Her eyes, Lukus noted with a shiver, were like the waters of an Arctic sea: not green, nor yet blue, but as cold as crackling ice-floes.

Cautiously, Lukus said, 'What was that you said?'

She replied, 'I said that I saw you leaving the Wasteland Eldorado. In one hell of a hurry.' Then she grinned, and it seemed as if the Arctic eyes were touched fleetingly by a warmer breeze. 'And now it's my turn to apologize for my language.' She cocked her head. 'Why don't we retire to the café and, over coffee, work out how you're going to get me back my hotel?'

Her name was Lil Lavender. She drank her coffee like a man, took a thick beef sandwich with it, dripping with mustard. Afterwards she smoked a thin cigar held like a blacksmith, and only then did she begin talking.

'Like a fool, I walked away from the hotel that gave me a kind of living when

Wasteland died,' she said.

'What went wrong? With the town, not with your hotel.'

She shrugged. 'It was a natural death. The old drifter who hammered in a wooden stake and established a settlement there got it right, and got it wrong. A wasteland was what it was, but where he was wrong was in believing he could make a change. Edge of a desert, not a sensible place to grow crops or raise livestock, no other way of raising money. Somehow the damn place staggered on for Lord knows how many years. The end came eighteen months ago when the population was so reduced the saloon couldn't sell beer. I was broke, walked away. Same time as that, up north in the town of Pine Rivers, a dumb fool leading the council found religion and decided to ban gambling.'

'Can't be done,' Lukus said.

'It was tried, and it snatched the livelihood out from under one man's shiny boots. Blackjack Chancer. He didn't waste time waiting for policies to change. Wasteland was about to become a ghost town, so he rode south with a couple of loaded wagons, tossed my fine old furniture into the street and set up his tables in what had been the Homestead Hotel.'

'And if you'd hung on . . . ?'

She nodded grimly. 'Yeah, you'll know that life's loaded with ifs. The gambling ban in Pine Rivers was a mistake that didn't last more than six months. By then Chancer was all set up in Wasteland and had sucked others along in his wake. Overnight, it seemed, Wasteland was the place to be if you were a businessman looking for a killing, or a fool hell-bent on losing his shirt.'

'Which is what Chancer did a week ago,' Lukus said. 'Or just a small part of it, like a sleeve, maybe, or a few pearl buttons he won't miss.' He frowned. 'But what about you? Your hotel's been turned into a gambling joint. How do you make a living?'

'I run a rooming house on the other side of that stretch of ground that helped give Wasteland its name.'

'The town's main street?'

She pulled a face. 'That's what they call it. Cuts through town, as you saw, open to the wind, a barren playground for rabid cats and tumbleweed. But it suits me because I can keep an eye on Chancer.'

She was eyeing him with what seemed to be expectancy, and he nodded understanding.

'The way it worked out,' he said shrewdly, 'you ended up watching more than the Wasteland gambler.'

'You made that Sunday morning unusual, and exciting. I was in a rocking-chair on my gallery, clutching my third cup of coffee with both hands. Dozing, if you want the truth. Shaded from the hot sun, but oh so warm and comfortable. So I missed you coming in: then I was startled into wakefulness by the sound of shots and there you were, a tall man on a big roan horse.

Blazing away at the town marshal, then hightailing with what looked like a bundle of washing tucked between your thighs.'

Lukus nodded slowly. That Lil Lavender had watched him ride away with the stolen money that sunny Sunday morning was of no consequence. What worried him was that she seemed to have had no trouble tracking him down to the town of Nathan's Ford on the green banks of the Rio Grande, a good fifty miles south-west of Wasteland. If she could do that, so could Blackjack Chancer.

'You saw me leave Wasteland,' Lukus said thoughtfully, 'but how did you find me?'

'Old and worldly-wise is one way to describe me,' she said. 'Another is to call me lucky. Getting close to the man who had stolen my hotel meant walking into the Eldorado several times and losing a few dollars on his gambling tables. I was down to my last chips one particularly noisy night when shots rang out and a young man sprawled across the craps table. He scattered high-value chips and dice when he went down, turned green baize a glistening red with his blood. I was holding the dice in my sweaty palms, was close enough to get a look at his face.'

She paused, pursing her lips as Lukus turned pale. 'I'm also sharp-eyed; added to which, on that Sunday I was using a nice pair of ivory opera glasses.'

'Pulled me in close.'

'Close enough to have noticed a clear resemblance when you rode away with Blackjack Chancer's takings. Your hat flipped off, remember that? The hot sunlight was on your face, and it was like looking at a ghost.'

Lukus nodded. 'I can see where this is going.'

'That young gambler I saw had to be your brother. His body went from the Eldorado to the undertakers. A week after you robbed Chancer I got to thinking, and toddled off to ask questions. I was told that the kid's body had been collected by his brothers. To do that you had to give proof that he was your brother, and the law required that you provide full names and an address.'

'Surely in confidence?'

'Think of Blackjack Chancer's philosophy. Money talks, makes others do the same.'

For a while nothing more was said. Lil Lavender finished her cigar. The café was empty, the air filled with the fading aromas of frying food and cigarette smoke. The young owner was singing softly as she clattered dishes in the kitchen. Lukus rose, went behind the counter and refilled their cups with warm coffee, jingled coins loudly on the counter.

When he sat down again the perspiring young woman was out of the kitchen acknowledging his payment with a smile. Lil Lavender was watching him, and there was something in her gaze that brought an involuntary shiver.

'That's how you found me,' Lukus

said, 'so now we get to the why.'

'I told you, Lukus. I want your help to get back the hotel that is rightfully mine.'

'But why me?'

'You're a hard man, and that's the kind I need. Chancer employs a gunslinger named Fallon. Fallon was there when you stole Chancer's takings. If you could best that cold-eyed man, you can surely do it again.'

'But why should I risk a return to Wasteland? We got clean away with that gambling money because my clever brother outfaced the town marshal. If he can find me, Jed Crane's got a personal score to settle. He and his men set off in pursuit of shadows. When they came back down the trail they found a broken-down wagon still there, half in the a creek, a putrefying sheep lying stinking in an open coffin.'

'Oh, you'll go back all right,' Lil Lavender said, her voice suddenly as cold as her merciless blue eyes, 'because I'm a witness to what went on that

Sunday in Wasteland and I just love talking.'

Lukus stared hard at her. The meal was a cold leaden weight on his stomach. But he didn't feel sick, he felt angry, and mostly with himself.

'I should have walked away.'

'Or kicked me off the plank walk when you had the chance.'

'I'm too young to be an old fool, but that's the way I feel.' He drew a breath. 'I could call your bluff.'

'I'm not bluffing.'

'OK, let's say you've got me over a barrel. So what happens next?'

'We make a plan. But first of all we sleep. I'll find a room in the hotel. You'll be heading for home. No doubt you'll be up most of the night talking things over with your brother. Tell him about the threat hanging over your heads — after all, you're in this together. But also tell yourselves this: helping an old lady regain her property from the man you've already robbed blind will cause him more pain, and could be a lot of fun.'

With an exchange of looks showing as much expression as a wooden Indian, they pushed back their chairs and left the café. The young owner called a cheery farewell, which fell on stony silence. Outside in the evening cool Lukus didn't pause, didn't utter a word. His boots clattered on the boards as he swung away and headed for the livery barn.

Lil Lavender turned the opposite way. With an elegance that drew the eye of every passer-by, she strolled along the plank walk in the warm glow of oil lamps flickering under the darkening evening skies. The hotel was fifty yards from the café. Lil took a deep, appreciative breath of the cool air, then entered the dusty interior.

The reception desk was unmanned. Flowers wilted under the weak light from a hanging brass oil lamp. Lil went on through. She climbed the stairs to the room she had booked earlier. For what she was about to do, a split riding-skirt was unsuitable. She changed her clothes, donning black trousers and a shirt to match, over those a dark jacket. She put a small silver derringer pistol in the jacket's pocket. Then she returned to the lower floor.

It was, she decided as she waited in the shadowy entrance hall, a job well done. She always had been a good talker, and could be convincing when speaking the truth, gabbling complete nonsense or looking a person in the eye with a killer gaze as she told barefaced lies.

Well, some of what she had told Lukus was true, and that helped, didn't it? A smattering of the truth to create padding to hide the lies? So, yes, she had indeed watched Lukus Rheingold leave Wasteland with what turned out to be a bag of stolen cash, she had tracked him down to Nathan's Ford by slipping a silver dollar to a seedy undertaker and, if Lukus refused to cooperate, she'd happily sell him out to the

Wasteland marshal.

But that was as far as it went.

On that Sunday a week in the past she had observed Lukus's departure, not from her own small business premises but from the shaded gallery of a rooming house where for six months she'd been paying rent. And if Blackjack Chancer had thrown furniture out of Wasteland's run-down hotel into the dusty street, it had not been hers. For while she had done many things in a life packed with incident, owning a hotel of any kind, anywhere, was not one of them.

Her thoughts were interrupted. Out in the street, a horse snorted softly and she caught the slow clip-clop of hoofs. When she opened the hotel's front door and stepped out into the evening light, Lukus Rheingold was riding by on his big roan. He glanced her way. She waved, gave him a big smile.

Then Lil Lavender walked the few yards down to Bud Jennings's livery barn, collected her horse, and within minutes was riding back up the street in the settling dust of Lukus Rheingold's passing.

5

Kris Rheingold was still stripped to the waist but nearing the end of his log-splitting when he heard the clatter of hoofs. At first he thought it was the woman coming back, or Lukus returning from town. Then he realized there was more than one horse, and heard deep male voices. He buried the axe head in a log, stretched, wiped the sweat from his face and limped round the house, dragging his shirt on.

'Can I help you, gents?'

Two men, both out of the saddle and walking away from their horses. They halted at Kris's approach. One was big and muscular, with a mane of white hair and cold blue eyes. Kris smothered a curse, instantly on his guard. It was the man who had ridden with the Wasteland posse that caught up with the buckboard stranded at No End

71

Creek. Blackjack Chancer. The other was a tall, lean man with dead eyes and a worn six-gun; his restless hands were covered by black leather gloves. From the description given to him by Lukus, Kris knew this must be Fallon, the gunslinger who'd been riding shotgun in Chancer's office.

The big man looked Kris up and down and said, 'I'm looking for the Rheingold brothers.'

Kris nodded slowly, thought fast.

'You've found Kris Rheingold, but you've been misinformed. I don't have a brother.'

'Kris Rheingold?' The big man raised an eyebrow. 'Last time we met, there was a buckboard and a mule and you were Joe Martin. Limping then, limping now. A man with a game leg and a real bad memory.'

'The sudden appearance of a posse makes a man jumpy, puts him on his guard.' Kris shrugged, allowed himself a thin smile.

'But a convenient change of name

72

doesn't explain a missing brother,' Chancer said. 'My source tells me you had two. One's dead, the other alive and causing me a heap of trouble.'

'Your source was drunk, or made a stupid mistake. You'd better check his credentials.'

'If you remember the posse, you'll remember Jed Crane, marshal of Wasteland. An experienced lawman. Honest, not easily fooled.'

'Where the hell is Wasteland?'

'You still suffering from memory loss? Four weeks ago you let a buckboard slide into No End Creek. The posse was from Wasteland. Crane told you as much. What I'm saying is your brother is the man who robbed a gambling joint in Wasteland. He rode like a bat out of hell to join you, scrambled aboard that wagon carrying a sack of stolen money. My money.'

'Then disappeared into thin air?'

'You'd both gone when we came back down the trail, you and that mule. Zac, the Indian, he had it figured before that. Before we reached you your brother rode on, then came back with his horse splashing in the creek waters. Hid somewhere. Joined you when the coast was clear.'

Kris raised his eyebrows, deliberately looked around the yard, at the timber house with dislodged shingles on the roof, a wide-open front door from which all paint had long since been bleached by the sun.

'Does this look like a rich man's abode?'

The tall gunman's laugh was brittle, stones rattling in a rusty can. He shook his head at Chancer. 'We're wasting time, because we both know he's lying through his teeth. We walk in through that door, there'll be clear signs tell us more than one man lives here.' He grinned at Kris. 'So here's the truth: if you stick with those lies, you can bet your life you'll be doing it through a mouth has lost most of its teeth.'

'Fallon,' Chancer said, as if an explanation were needed, 'is a man you do not want to rile.'

'For the last time I don't have a brother. I was on my own with that buckboard, and I sure as hell know nothing about stolen money —'

'You're right,' the gunman cut in, 'that is the last time.' With a scornful glance at Kris's waist to show he'd noticed the absence of a gunbelt, of any kind of weapon, he casually drew his six-gun. 'Into the *abode*, feller. Any wrong move, I'll put a bullet in your one good leg.'

The big man with the flowing white hair was already moving, pushing impatiently past Kris and into the house. When Kris followed — acutely aware of the gunman crowding him, of the raw smell of his sweat — he saw Chancer prowling, looking around and at once taking note of the breakfast dishes on the table: two greasy plates, two tin cups. As Kris stood watching, Chancer moved past the table to study framed tintypes above shelves on the rear wall. One was of a young man and woman with three boys, toddlers; a second showed the adults, now less upright and with greying hair. In this image they were flanked by two young men.

'Ma and Pa are dead,' Kris said, watching Chancer. 'So's my kid brother, Davy. He's been dead a month. Lukus left home years ago, that's why he's not in that picture. None of us ever had any word from him. Makes what I said a lie, but a small one; in a sense I really don't have a brother.'

Without warning he was pushed hard from behind. He hit the edge of the table with his thighs. The tin cups wobbled and clattered to the floor, spilling coffee dregs. When Kris turned, open-mouthed, he was hit in the face with a bony fist encased in a black leather glove. The gunman's wide shoulders put weight into the blow. Kris saw brightly flashing stars, heard a ringing in his ears. He staggered numbly backwards and was caught under the arms by Chancer.

'There's a corral out back,' the

76

gunman said, rubbing his fist, 'empty 'cept for one horse and one pesky mule. Slender evidence, for sure, but put that mule with a missing buckboard and what Chancer's been saying sounds good to me. So what we're looking for — in addition to the missing brother — is a pile of banknotes stinking of a long-dead sheep.' He grinned. 'Got to hand it to you, that was a neat trick — '

Kris Rheingold exploded into action. He twisted at the waist, drove his right elbow back hard into Chancer's belly. The big gambling man's hands fell away. He bent double, gasping for breath. Kris used the recoil to swing his arm up and over and slam his fist into the sharp angle of the gunman's jaw. Fallon's eyes glazed.

Then Kris was swarming all over him, throwing punches into his belly, his ribs, both sides of his gaunt face. Fallon fell backwards into the table. It rocked, then tipped over. A chair splintered as the gunman fell heavily, but his eyes had cleared.

Now he came up off the floor like a thin, coiled spring. Kris was closing in. The gunman swung a kick. The sharp toe of his boot connected with Kris's kneecap. Pain sliced through his leg. It buckled. His crippled leg could not take the weight. He fell awkwardly.

Again Chancer caught him, but now the big man was angry. Still breathless, he turned and muscled Kris up against a wall alongside an oak dresser. Kris's head cracked against the woodwork. Dizziness swept over him in a sickening wave. The leg Fallon had kicked ached from hip to ankle. He concentrated on it, willing it to hold him upright. Chancer stared into his eyes. He held Kris against the wall with the flat of his hands, then smiled coldly and stepped away.

'We're not fools, Rheingold. You can rage, throw punches, but everything we've seen ties with what Jed Crane's told me, what I saw for myself at No End Creek.'

Kris could find no words for what he

knew was a futile argument. His knee was red hot. He winced as he shifted his weight, then braced himself with his back against the wall as Fallon came at him in a rush.

The gunman, teeth red with blood, reached him in two long strides. His swinging fist came up from the floor and cracked against Kris's jaw. It was as if a lamp, the only illumination in the room, had been suddenly extinguished, leaving nothing but blackness.

He could feel a dislodged tooth with his tongue, but not too easily because any movement of his mouth sent pain lancing from his jaw to his ear. There was the coppery taste of blood, the smell of cigarette smoke. Voices sounded, close but indistinct because his head was swimming, ears buzzing. His pulse felt like the faltering ticking of a very old watch with a weak mainspring. He kept his eyes shut, swallowing nausea. Then he was kicked hard in the ribs. He clenched his teeth against a groan. His eyes creaked open.

He was lying close to the open fireplace with its cold iron stove and stone chimney; he recalled hitting his head on the way down before the blackness closed in. Even as he was contemplating how much effort would be needed to regain his feet, whether he had one good leg to stand on if he made it, the problem was solved. Chancer, the gambling man, used both big hands to drag him erect without any noticeable effort, and again slammed him against the wall.

'Where's your brother?'

'I don't know. He left home years ago . . . '

The words trailed away. The familiar room was blurred, the furniture too dark, the sunlight, spilling in through the still-open door, was too bright and shimmering. All that was holding him upright was the big man leaning against him, stiff-armed, hand planted on his chest.

'Where's my money?'

'Jesus Christ,' Kris said huskily, 'what money?'

Chancer stepped away. Kris took an involuntary, limping forward step, felt his crippled leg begin to give way. Then the gunman took over. Again Kris was slammed back against the wall. Then, head down, rolling his shoulders like a prizefighter skilled at infighting, Fallon began punching. He used both fists, rocked Kris's head from side to side with short, jabbing blows. He was in so close that Kris was held upright. Too weak to fight back, he was forced to soak up the punishment as his senses reeled.

The punches were vicious, their weight carefully judged. Bony knuckles inside the leather gloves slashed at areas where there was little flesh between skin and bone, causing agony. One punch broke Kris's nose. He heard the crunch of shattered bone, felt the spurt of hot blood. The blood soaked Fallon's gloves. He brought the attack down and began pounding a succession of thumping blows into the soft mid-section under Kris's ribs.

Kris couldn't breathe.

And somewhere there was Chancer.

'Where's your brother? Where's my money? Where's your brother? Where's my money? Where's your brother? Where's my money . . . ?'

Kris felt himself floating. The cruel beating was taking its toll. His mind was drifting, floating free of his tortured body and into blessed unconsciousness. He knew that — but that was where coherent thought ended. The gunman could no longer hold him upright.

Kris went down under the unrelenting rain of Fallon's blows. His last memory was of the disembodied voice of Chancer, the gambling man, warning him that what he had experienced was just the start and that unless he saw sense and came clean he'd likely spend the rest of his life in a chair with wheels, being spoon-fed by a nurse.

Then, feeling the start of a broad grin that was surely pure imagination, Kris Rheingold again lost interest.

6

There was, Lukus decided as he took the roan out of Nathan's Ford and headed home, only one thing to do with the money they had stolen. In the morning he would dig it up from the place where it was buried, and deliver it to Frank Bellard, the town marshal. Tell him they'd found it, stumbled across it when halting for a smoke, a tarpaulin-wrapped bundle lying in the fringe of woods off the trail just outside Nathan's Ford. He'd hope that their dead brother's notoriety hadn't left them tarred with the same brush, or Bellard with the sour taste of suspicion and a reluctance to believe what was a pretty tall story.

For when both parents died, young Davy Rheingold had gone wild. Not out-and-out bad. But while Kris earned the money needed to put food on the table, working for long stretches on nearby ranches, young Davy spent his time in town, drinking, gambling, and raising hell. More than once he had ended up in Frank Bellard's jail. More than once he had been bailed out by Kris, using money they could ill afford. Not once had Davy promised to reform.

Indeed, it had been the conviction that what he was doing would one day make them rich that had taken him on the ride north-east across the Big Bend Desert to Wasteland. By this time Lukus was back home. And, Lukus thought ruefully, they'd done nothing to stop Davy because both he and Kris were hoping that losing cash in a rigged game in Blackjack Chancer's Eldorado would teach young Davy a lesson he would never forget.

It had turned out to be a lesson that would forever be there to torment the kid's stupid brothers, Lukus thought bitterly. Not for the first time, he thanked the Lord that their parents were dead.

In the warm light of late evening Lukus pulled the big roan in under a cottonwood, lit a cigarette and sat in the saddle brooding.

Who or what was Lil Lavender? Was her toughness the brave façade put up by a woman fighting to regain what was rightfully hers? Or was she tough all through, born wicked; beneath that hard exterior shell was a black heart beating wickedly? Behind those ice-blue eyes was there a brain that was cool and calculating? Certainly Lukus believed that she would not hesitate to give his name to the Wasteland marshal. In truth, it didn't matter. In a while Lukus would tell Kris how he and the woman had met and what they'd discussed, then he'd sit back and watch his younger brother struggle not to say *What did I tell you?'*

Kris had been against the robbery from the start. 'Stealing Chancer's money,' he'd said, 'is piling wrong on top of wrong. It won't bring Davy back, and it'll cause us a heap of trouble.' So he would scoff at any thought of a return to Wasteland to help a complete stranger. He'd also grimace at the idea of handing over the stolen cash to Nathan's Ford's marshal. As far as Kris was concerned, buried was buried. Leave the damned stuff under the turf to rot, he'd said — more than once, and even now Lukus had the sneaking suspicion his brother was right.

Nevertheless . . .

Lukus's mind was already made up. It was a decision forced on him by the threat hanging over his head. In the morning he would walk into Frank Bellard's office and dump the stinking, tarpaulin-wrapped bundle on his desk. Then he would seek out the elegant, formidable Lil Lavender and tell her that the money had been returned, her threat no longer held any weight. Chancer was miles away. If she wanted her hotel back she'd have to make the ride home, then go tell her story to Wasteland's marshal, Jed Crane.

Even at that point Lukus couldn't see

what should have been blindingly obvious: that if Lil Lavender's story was true, Jed Crane and the denizens of Wasteland would have been eagerly following it from the moment her furniture hit the street. Instead of taking his thinking the one step further that would have saved him what Kris called a heap of trouble, Lukus flicked his cigarette into a patch of damp grass, then pulled out on to the trail and continued on his way home.

★   ★   ★

When he was just half a mile away from the small Rheingold spread he knew with certainty that there was a rider behind him on the trail. The sun had sunk low in the west. The skies over Mexico had been painted from a rich palette of dazzling reds and golds that dimmed the face of a rising quarter-moon. The shadows of dusk were long and deceptive.

A few seconds spent scanning his

back trail revealed nothing, but the sound of hoofs had come clear and sharp to his ears through the still air. One horse, or two? He couldn't be sure, but did realize with a twinge of anger that those sounds must have been there in his subconscious for some time. He also recalled, now, that when he had stopped for his cigarette the sounds had ceased.

But who were they, and what did they want? In the gathering gloom, Lukus smiled bitterly. He'd already worked out that if Lil Lavender could track him to his home town, so could Blackjack Chancer and his pet gunslinger. It was beginning to look highly probable that those suspicions had become a hard fact. Lukus was now willing to bet his shirt that Chancer and the tall gunman had been somewhere in Nathan's Ford, had watched him leave, then waited for dusk before hitting the trail in pursuit.

This time when Lukus pulled off the trail he chose a small copse he knew well, guiding the roan down a gentle cottonwood-shrouded slope to a hollow where a stagnant pool lay coated with green moss. That position, he knew, gave him a clear view through the trees to the trail while yet affording some cover. He dismounted. The roan moved along the edge of the water with trailing reins and began to graze.

All was quiet. The undergrowth rustled as a small animal fled from the intruders. Somewhere close by an owl hooted, then flew away with a flap of wings. The hoofbeats that had alerted Lukus were silent. The pursuers had heard him stop, and done the same. He knew that couldn't last. The men following would be listening. They would wait just so long. Suspicion would eat away at patience, and they would come in hard and fast to find out what the hell Lukus was doing.

Lukus slipped his Winchester out of his saddle boot, jacked a shell into the breech so that no later sound would betray his presence. Then he moved silently past the dank water and up the slope from the hollow. He waited patiently, among the trees a couple of yards back from the trail. He could feel his heart beating, hear the soft murmur of his pulse in his ears.

Then that soft hissing was overwhelmed as a rider came around a bend in the trail, in the night stillness the rapid beat of hoofs like the rattle of sticks on a Thanksgiving kettledrum.

Lukus eased back, his eyes narrowed. He brought the rifle up at his shoulder. One rider, not two. Frowning, he watched as the flying horseman hammered down the trail. The line he was taking would bring him close to Lukus's position. The skies had darkened. The moon was a wan quarter-disc floating behind hazy cloud. In that poor light Lukus could see little more than a dark figure on a racing horse. A black coat was unfastened. It flared like a highwayman's cloak driven by the wind. In the shadows cast by a black hat the pale face was unrecognizable.

Not Chancer. Fallon, then? Possibly. A lean, mean gunslinger, a killer bearing a grudge.

The rider was almost upon him. Uncertain, loath to kill a man in cold blood, Lukus tipped the rifle barrel towards the skies and fired two spaced shots high above the rider's head. He was hoping for a reaction of some kind. The result was breathtakingly effective.

The shock of the twin detonations and the dazzling muzzle-flashes startled the fast-moving horse. Its head jerked up, its free-flowing stride faltered. Distracted, it stepped in an unseen pothole. Its right foreleg snapped like a dry twig and the horse went down in a crunching tumble that sent the rider over its head to hit the ground hard, bounce like a rag doll, then lie still.

The horse, snorting, thrashing, struggled to rise. Then, whinnying pitifully, it flopped back. Its chest was heaving, its warm breath a misty cloud on the chill night air.

But more than all of that, Lukus had

seen something that caused his heart to lurch, his mouth turn dry with shock. The moon had drifted clear of the veil of cloud. As the rider went down the black hat had flipped loose and rolled into the undergrowth. What was left to Lukus's appalled gaze was an ominously still figure with a pale face pressed against the hard earth of the trail and partly shrouded by a mane of blonde-grey hair.

The woman's eyes were closed, their lashes dark against the pallor. She made no movement. Lukus crashed through the bushes that had been his shield, and jacked a shell into the rifle's breech. He approached the crippled horse, out of habit murmuring words of comfort that had no meaning at such a time. Then he pressed the rifle's muzzle against the animal's head, and pulled the trigger.

Death was instantaneous. As the sound of the bullet's detonation faded and the night was again still, Lukus glanced across at the other silent figure. Searching in vain for any stirring of that motionless form cloaked in black, he was struck by the awful conviction that on that rutted track he was now looking at two dead bodies.

7

Lil Lavender was out cold, but seemed to be breathing. Her cheek was pressed against the dirt, long eyelashes dark against her pallor. Her grey hair was a stringy mess soaked with blood, but even minor scalp wounds bleed as if an artery has been severed. When Lukus felt with unsteady fingers for a pulse in the warm flesh of her throat, there was an immediate rush of relief: the woman was alive.

He lifted her head, moved her hand under her face as a cushion. Then he whispered something warm and comforting close to her ear, told her he'd be back, and jogged off the trail, down into the hollow for his horse. There, kneeling in the damp grass, he broke through the green-scummed surface of the pool and soaked his bandanna in the cold water.

Back on the trail with his horse, again leaving the reins trailing, he knelt by the woman. It took just a few applications of the wet cloth to her forehead to bring a flutter to those long eyelashes, then a sudden startled return to consciousness and immediate awareness.

She was wearing a thin scarf around her neck, as dark as the rest of her attire. Again Lukus slipped his fingers in against the warm pulsing of her throat. He gently slipped off the thin material, folded it into a soft pad.

'Hold this against your head,' he said. 'I think the bleeding's stopped, but if you press firmly it'll make sure.'

She complied, wincing. Lukus left her to it. Moving quickly, he untied the rope from his saddle and secured it to the horn. Using the roan's strength, he dragged the dead horse off the trail and into the long grass. Then he returned to Lil Lavender.

Some colour had returned to her cheeks. She hooked her arm in his and used his strength to get back on her feet. She was as weak as a newborn calf.

'Damn you, Rheingold,' she said shakily. 'All the luck's going your way. Leave me to bleed to death and your troubles are over.'

'But if you die now, I'll never get to the truth.'

Suddenly she was wary, as if realizing her condition could make her careless with words. She managed a wan smile, but her eyes were narrowed against weakness and pain. Lukus got her up on to the roan, then walked the few hundred yards to the house alongside the horse and its dazed burden. The sight of his home brought another surge of relief. That lasted until he had tied the horse, helped Lil out of the saddle and up the steps, and led her slowly across the gallery.

From a distance Lukus had observed the dim light in the front room. It had been like a beacon, guiding him and the injured woman to sanctuary. But his boots thudded hollowly on the gallery's boards. Under his weight a rusty nail squealed like a young pig.

The light was extinguished.

Lukus stopped dead. He looked at Lil. Her head was bowed. Clutching his arm she was suffering in silence, aware of nothing outside her own bruised body.

Cautiously, Lukus continued across the gallery. He touched the front door. It swung open. Lukus felt the hairs on the back of his neck prickle. Clearly he could smell the coal oil burned by the lamp. But beneath it, barely detectable, there was a raw, coppery smell.

'Something's wrong,' he whispered.

'What . . . ?'

Speaking softly, he said, 'I want you to sit over there, and keep quiet.'

He led her to his pa's old rocking-chair. It sagged when she sat down, rocked gently, the old wooden runners creaking. She breathed a ragged sigh of relief and rested her head against the tall back. She was watching him. In the moonlight leaking in under the over-hanging roof her blue eyes were pale, almost luminous.

Treading carefully, Lukus returned to stand with his back flattened against the wall alongside the open door. He eased his six-gun out of its holster, then paused for thought.

The smell told Lukus blood had been spilled in that room. The men who had done the bloodletting were still inside. It had to be Blackjack Chancer and the gunman, Fallon. They'd heard the rifle shots, heard Lukus and Lil Lavender ride in on the roan.

One of them must have blown out the lamp. They would by now have backed off into the deepest shadowy corners — one man on either side of the darkened room. Their guns would be trained on the lighter rectangle of the open doorway. Anyone who stepped into that narrow opening would be revealed instantly. A dark shape would loom against a backdrop of pale moonlight. A sitting duck, to be riddled with bullets.

But, as events in the Wasteland

gambling joint had proved, Lukus Rheingold was no sitting duck.

There was a window on either side of the Rheingold house's front door. One was at Lil Lavender's back as she sat in the old rocking-chair. It was to the other window that Lukus went. Acutely aware of the danger he would face in crossing that open door, he took the long way round.

He went back across the gallery like a wraith, touched Lil Lavender's shoulder and whispered, 'Stay there.' Then he vaulted over the gallery's side rail. He swished through the short grass in the deep shade at the side of the house. The back yard was redolent with the smell of sap from cooling logs split by Kris in the afternoon heat. Lukus's presence was detected by the mule in the corral. It brayed softly — a sound Lukus welcomed. It would be heard by the men in the house, and cause some confusion. They'd know there had to be a back door. But which door would Lukus use?

The short walk round the other side of the house brought him to the rail on that side of the gallery. This one he climbed over with caution. Even so, the age-old wood cracked loudly. Wincing, knowing he now had to move fast, Lukus holstered his six-gun. Then he stepped a couple of paces back from the front wall of the house and launched himself at the window.

He tucked himself into a ball and exploded into the room, carrying with him shattered glass and the window's broken framework. He fell heavily, took his weight on his hands, rolled. Plates and cups were sent clattering across the hard floor. Uncoiling, he flung himself sideways. He slammed a hand down on a broken table leg and felt a splinter drive deep into his palm. He instinctively pulled his hand away, lost balance and fell again. His shoulder hit a chair, lying on its side. His arm went numb.

Lukus bit his lip against the pain. The blood on his hand was warm and liquid. He was on the floor, curled up amid furniture that had been in disarray even before his explosive entrance sent cups and plates clattering that had already been on the floor. He had burst into the house with enough noise to stampede a herd of buffalo — to no reaction. No six-guns had spat flame. No bullets had drilled into the floor or punched bloody holes in his flesh.

He was alone in the room.

Taking a deep breath, Lukus climbed to his feet. Laughter bubbled. He felt like a fool who'd thrashed about on the floor of that darkened room for no damn reason.

Then the laughter died. Brightening moonlight flooding through the doorway to form a pool on the littered dirt floor was suddenly blocked. A dark figure stepped into the room. He was holding a glittering pistol.

8

Lukus stooped, silently scooped up a tin cup and flung it in a high arc across the room. It smacked against the far wall, fell and bounced. The man with the gun drew in a hissing breath. He swung in that direction with the pistol raised. Lukus took three crunching steps across the room and pounced.

He took the man from behind. One hand snapped down on the extended wrist, holding it still. His other arm whipped over the man's shoulder. Bending it at the elbow, he locked his forearm hard up against the exposed throat. The man choked, began to struggle. Lukus tightened his grip, making breathing impossible. He increased pressure on the wrist, shook it furiously and heard the pistol fall to the floor. He sensed the man's strength leaking away like water through a rusted tin can, felt muscles slacken.

Suddenly he was holding the man's weight as his legs began to buckle. But it was a feint, a trick. A foot was lifted and stabbed backwards, raking Lukus's shin. Then the man stamped on his instep. Reaction to the agony caused Lukus to bend forward. He came hard up against the man's back, his face buried in hair.

Long hair. Soft hair, but soft hair already stiffening with drying blood.

Mouth tight, Lukus released his grip. He stepped back. An elbow drove hard under his ribs, and Lil Lavender swung on him, her face furious in the gloom. She bent and scooped up the pistol. It was, Lukus saw, a tiny, double-barrelled gambler's gun. Without pause, she levelled it at his chest.

'If I didn't need you so bad,' she said, 'I'd finish you off now.'

'With a derringer? What in God's name were you hoping to do with that toy?'

'At close range it's as good as a Gatling.'

'And I was damn close to breaking your neck.'

'Many have tried,' she said, visibly struggling for calm.

Her words were defiant, but her voice was weak. The fierce struggle after the fall from her horse had taken what remained of her strength. Breathing was difficult. One trembling hand was touching her throat where Lukus had clamped his arm. She swayed. Lukus took her arm before she could fall and settled her in an overstuffed chair.

'That was your third chance to get out from under,' she said, 'and again you didn't take it.' Beneath the tangle of blonde-grey hair her blue eyes were now shrewd. 'An owlhoot with scruples, or maybe it's a guilty conscience. No matter. I came in to save you because I heard what sounded like a barroom brawl. But you're alone in here. What the hell were you doing?'

Her powers of recovery were remarkable, and she was not content to sit. She twisted in the soft chair and looked around the wrecked room. When she stretched out an arm, glaring at him, Lukus helped her to her feet. She held his shoulder, then let go as he moved away towards the back of the room.

He stepped carefully, for the fight — and, hellfire, it must have been some battle — had wrecked furniture, turned the room's once-familiar layout into a trap for the unwary.

'We know someone blew out the light,' Lil said. 'We both saw it, so where are they?'

But Lukus was shaking his head. The oil lamp was in its usual place, on a high shelf. When he picked it up it was warm, but by its weight he knew it was empty.

'We were fooled,' he said. 'I'd say the lamp was left lit to guide us, but it ran out of oil.'

'Guide us to what?'

The light in the room was too dim to

see anything clearly. Lukus struck a match. In the flare of light he found a stub of candle in a holder, and lit that. The wick sputtered. The flame wavered, caught. Lukus held the candle high.

'Holy Christ!' Lil Lavender said.

But again Lukus was not listening. His nervous breathing, the tremor in his hand, were causing the candle's flame to flicker. He used both hands to hold it steady, stared in horror. A tintype had been torn from the wall and tossed aside. A sheet of paper ripped from a book Lukus's pa had used for accounts was suspended from the nail. Someone had written on it, using a pointed stick dipped in blood:

A word of warning. I have your brother. If you want to see him alive, there's a price on his head. When you've figured out how much he's worth, come talk to me, and come alone.

9

It was early morning when Lukus Rheingold saddled his roan and headed for town. The thin mist floating in from the Rio Grande was like a threadbare white carpet across grassland sparkling with dew. It touched the trail with thin skeins that curled about the roan's legs, there to be cut to fast-fading ribbons by the horse's flashing hoofs.

Lukus rode hard and fast, even though he knew that haste, driven by the fury smouldering inside him, would resolve no problems. The disbelief and sheer panic that had hit him like a hammer blow when, in the flickering candlelight, he saw the scrawled, bloody writing, had tormented him throughout the long, sleepless night. That, and his growing suspicions about Lil Lavender, the woman who the warning shots fired from his Winchester had damn near killed.

She had suggested he had a guilty conscience, perhaps little knowing she was perilously close to the truth. The worry was that the remark could have been a poisoned dart fired by someone in the know. Someone, Lukus had been quick to note, who had been more than willing to pick up the gambler's gun and threaten to shoot.

But they had been the words of a woman almost out on her feet in that wrecked living room. Lukus had carried the candle in one hand and helped the bruised and exhausted woman into the bedroom that had belonged to his parents. There she had slept the sleep of the dead.

She had still been sleeping when, in the grey light of dawn, Lukus had pushed his suspicions to one side and crept into her room. She was, after all was said and done, his only ally, albeit one holding a threat over his head. So there in the bedroom's half-light he had leaned close to the still form and whispered instructions that he hoped had registered somewhere, even if only in her subconscious.

Then, backing out of the room, he had slammed out of the house.

He was more than halfway to Nathan's Ford before he recalled his intention of taking the stolen money to Marshal Frank Bellard. The thought crossed his mind in a flash, and was instantly dismissed as no longer relevant. Less than twelve hours ago that tarpaulin parcel had been a rod for his and Kris's backs. Now it had become a hole card, held in reserve to be played only if there was no other way of saving Kris's life.

He hit town in a rush, pushing the lathered roan down the main street to the astonishment, then frowning concern of Will Travis, who was polishing the brass plate on the wall alongside his office's open door. Unaware of the lawyer's worried scrutiny, Lukus rode through the awakening town and pulled up outside the jail, dust swirling in the early-morning sunlight. He tumbled from the saddle, loose-tied the reins to the hitch rail, then stamped his way into the marshal's office.

Frank Bellard was long, lean and wolfish. He wore a sweat-stained Stetson that he had never been known to doff, and his straggling, tobacco-stained moustache hid both corners of a mouth that was quick to smile. He was rarely fazed. When Lukus burst into the office he saw the lawman raise an eyebrow without bothering to look up. His long legs were stretched out, his booted feet up on the edge of an oak desk scarred by his spurs. Wire-framed glasses, badly misshapen, were perched on the end of his long nose. His keen blue eyes were studying a creased document.

Still not looking up, he said, 'Glad you could come in, Lukus. You must have read my mind: you've saved me the trouble of a ride out.'

Lukus, chest heaving, mind in turmoil, was halted in his tracks by the pointed remark.

'You know something I don't?'

Bellard let the paper fall face down on the desk, alongside his Colt revolver. He stroked his moustache, grinned crookedly.

'Hell, Lukus, you know as well as I do that's one of those questions can't be answered unless both parties come clean. You look like you're bursting with something or other, so why don't you go first?'

'I was in town yesterday, rode home in the evening to find the house a mess. Living room wrecked, place splashed with blood. There was a note' — he took a deep breath, steadied himself — 'there was a note pinned to the wall, written in blood. Kris's been taken, against his will. I get him back if I pay a ransom.'

Bellard raised both eyebrows in disbelief. 'Now why in the world would anyone take young Kris Rheingold?'

'Are you stupid, Bellard? I told you, I can get him back but it's going to cost me.'

'But you Rheingold's ain't got any money. Or am I wrong there? You've not been around these parts too long, so I don't know you all that well. Did you bring cash with you when you came home, keep a pile stashed away these past six months? Or are these fellers considering wealth suddenly . . . acquired, shall we say?' He cocked a questioning eyebrow, waited. When no answer was forthcoming he said, 'And who are these fellers, anyway? You ain't said, but if you're askin' me to go hunt them down, I need to know.'

Lukus shook his head. He wheeled away, stood staring at the window and the early sun slanting across the town's roofs, casting hard-edged shadows across the street. He looked for reassurance in the familiar scene, found none; he sensed from the marshal's words that Bellard knew a damn sight more than he was letting on.

It had always been on the cards that fading Wanted dodgers would be lying around or stuffed in dusty drawers. Had Bellard passed a hot afternoon idly sifting through them, been shocked at recognizing a familiar face carrying another name?

Struggling for composure, Lukus swung around and glared at the marshal.

'I've reported a crime,' he said. 'Bandying words gets us nowhere, leaves Kris in danger. Are you going to sit there all day?'

'You ain't asked me why I was about to ride out to your place.'

'I'm not interested.'

'You should be, because you saved both of us a ride.' Bellard sighed, and with one finger he rotated the revolver on the desk so that the butt was close to his big hand. 'I was about to bring you in, son. You're under arrest for robbery with what the complainant calls a certain amount of violence.'

'What complainant?'

113

'Feller called Blackjack Chancer.'

'Fancy name for someone lying through his teeth.'

'That's as maybe. Fact is he rode all the way from Wasteland to do his lying. Came in here all hot and dusty. Least I can do is follow up his story.'

Lukus listened to the words, his muscles tense; within him there was an overpowering urge to turn and get the hell away from there. Then behind him he heard heavy footsteps crossing the plank walk. The room darkened as the doorway was blocked by the newcomer.

'That's Smoky Willis you hear,' Bellard said, watching Lukus's face. 'He's a powerful feller, my deputy, as you well know, so right now you've got no way out. I'd be much obliged if you'd take your pistol out of leather using just a finger and thumb, and lay it on the desk alongside my Colt.'

Not moving, Lukus said, 'Robbery with some violence?' He laughed harshly. 'What the hell did I do?'

'Held up this aforementioned Black-jack Chancer in his Wasteland Eldorado. Made a mess of his colleague's arm with that six-gun you're carrying. Forced the gambling man to fill a sack with hard-earned cash.'

'I've been to Wasteland once, and only once.' Lukus paused. 'You know that. Chancer's Eldorado is where my kid brother was murdered. Me and Kris, we collected his remains.'

'The undertaker who took care of young Davy's body on that terrible night is the man who one month later saw you walk your horse around the back of Chancer's place. He was driving his hearse, hung around long enough to hear shots. Watched you leave, saw what you were carrying. Saw you fire your pistol at the approaching town marshal.'

'My word against his. The sun addled his brains.'

'He was out on the street the same time as Crane and Chancer. Three men, same tale to tell.'

'I walked in here hoping for some help,' Lukus said. 'I lost one brother. Now Blackjack Chancer has taken Kris.'

'I'm not saying he's going about it the right way, or even if it's him did the taking, but the man wants his money.'

'You're arresting me for a crime committed in a town fifty miles away. Can you do that? You're town marshal, here in Nathan's Ford. It's not your responsibility.'

'The defeat of the lawless element in society doesn't recognize boundaries,' Bellard said, his eyes suddenly cold. 'I'm taking you in, Lukus, and you'll be locked in a cell until Marshal Jed Crane collects you. Give up your gun, now.'

Lukus spun away from the desk. Expecting the deputy to be crowding him from behind, he had his left arm raised as a block covering his jaw and was cocking his right fist for the telling blow. But Smoky Willis, a veteran of countless barroom brawls, had kept space between them. His bulk was blocking the doorway. Lukus was caught in no-man's-land between two armed lawmen. Rooted to the spot, he calculated the odds, didn't like them, so began pushing his luck.

Not turning, he said, 'I'm walking out of here, Bellard. The only way you can stop me is by shooting me in the back.' Assuming an arrogance he did not feel, he took a pace forward, then another, saw the big deputy frown, tense.

'If you're right,' Lukus went on, 'I took a few dollars from a flashy gambler who got one of my brothers killed.' Another step, and he was closing in on Willis. The deputy was hesitating, unwilling to act, waiting anxiously for a sign from the marshal.

Lukus grinned. 'A petty crime, Bellard, that's all it was,' he said, 'and the silence I'm hearing tells me you're troubled. You know if you kill me it's likely my remaining brother will die. Do you want his death on your conscience for the rest of your life?'

Even as he spoke he took one more step. It was all he needed. He was a tall man with a long reach and, as fast as a striking snake, his left hand flashed out. He took a grip on Willis's shirt front. Twisted. Held him. Brought a wicked right hand around in a looping punch. He put his shoulder behind the blow. His fist cracked against the angle of Willis's jaw. The deputy's eyes rolled. He went down, smashing the open door back against the wall.

Behind him there was a muted grunt that could have been astonishment. It was cut short. Then there was the sound of a six-gun being cocked. The hairs on his neck prickling, Lukus took a fast step forward. It carried him into the sunlight flooding the doorway. The light and the heat hit him. Open space and freedom were one short step away.

It was a step he would never take. The six-gun blast when it came was a shock that set his ears ringing. The bullet gouged into the floor between his

118

booted feet, showering the dazed deputy with the dust of years.

'You're trying my patience,' Frank Bellard said, and Lukus could hear the anger in his voice. 'Use the good sense you were born with, feller. Turn around, hand over that pistol and walk nice and easy to a cell. Forget my conscience. You do as I say, or I'm lifting my aim and planting a shot somewhere that'll put an end to this business, and your life.'

10

When Lil Lavender tottered out of the bedroom on unsteady legs she found herself in a living room sweltering in the midday heat. The wreckage remained mostly as she remembered seeing it by the light of the flickering candle, the lingering stink of drying blood sickening in the close atmosphere. She opened the front door, stepped out to breathe deeply of the fresh air, looked across the sagging gallery to the hitch rail and beyond that to open country shimmering under near-white skies and split by the trail into town.

There was no sign of Lukus Rheingold, either in the house or elsewhere, but at the back of Lil's mind something was nagging, something important. Try as she might, she could not drag those thoughts to the surface.

Over breakfast, she decided, that's when all will be revealed; and she wandered into a big kitchen where a stove that presumably was never allowed to go out was adding to the oppressive heat.

It was the hot coffee that jogged her memory — her second cup — when she was sitting relaxing. Lukus had come into her room, very early. She had been aware of his presence, but was emerging sluggishly from a sleep so deep that she had neither the strength nor the inclination to open her eyes. He had bent close to her, whispered in her ear, and it was those words that now emerged to intrigue her.

'If I'm not back by midday,' he'd said, 'ride into town and go see lawyer Will Travis.'

All right, Lil thought, *but what the hell are you up to, Lukus Rheingold?* Then she looked unseeingly across the rim of her coffee cup and shook her head in chagrin. It was now well past that midday deadline, and her horse was lying dead in the long grass.

But of course, she thought, there's always the mule out there in the corral — and thanking the Lord that her thinking was unimpaired, her injuries not as debilitating as she had feared, she dissolved into bubbling laughter at the thought of the ride that lay ahead.

★ ★ ★

Will Travis was leaning against the wall enjoying a cigar in the warm shade outside his office when Frank Bellard walked up the street. The marshal was frowning, and his eyes were not on the lawyer but on the elegant woman in the dusty black clothing with ominous stains. Out in the middle of the street, she was having difficulty with a mule.

The mule was stubbornly refusing to move. Amused onlookers were shouting advice. Caught in the sun's direct rays, the woman was unable to escape the searing heat. Her face was red and glistening with perspiration as she kicked the mule furiously with her heels.

'Ain't that the Rheingold mule she's astride?' Bellard said when he reached the lawyer.

'If it is, that explains the trouble she's having,' Travis said with a grin. 'It's more accustomed to pulling a buckboard.'

'Which, as I recall, went missing about a week ago.'

Travis looked sharply at the marshal. 'What's going on, Frank?'

But Bellard wasn't listening. He'd stepped into the street, and was out in the bright sun talking to the woman. She nodded and slipped out of the saddle. Bellard caught her arm, beckoned to a ragged kid who was on the fringe of the crowd, and gestured to the mule. The youngster ran across and leaped into the saddle. The mule snorted and obligingly, infuriatingly, began to move. Bellard helped the woman across the street's ruts, up on to the plank walk and into Travis's office.

She slumped weakly into the lawyer's swivel-chair. Travis brought her a glass of cool water. She downed it in a series of gulps. Then she sighed, sat back, and managed a smile.

'At least the stubborn beast stopped where I wanted it to,' she said.

'In the middle of the street?' Travis said, straight-faced.

'No, level with your office. My name is Lil Lavender. If you're Will Travis, it's you I was coming to see.'

'On Lukus Rheingold's mule,' Bellard said. He was standing back against the bookshelves, eyes bright in the shadows.

'My horse broke a leg. It's a long story, and most of it I don't understand. What I do know is that before Lukus left — and that was very early — he told me to come and see Mr Travis if he was late returning.'

'What happened to your head?'

Instinctively, Lil touched the wound. The bleeding had stopped hours ago, but she had not yet washed her greying hair. It was matted, clotted with dried blood. She knew that her jacket, too, was a giveaway: to any lawman the stains would immediately be recognizable.

'It has a place in that long story,' she said, 'without being an essential part of it.'

'Lukus is in jail, Miss Lavender.'

'Lil.'

'Same story, Lil. He's committed a crime, and he'll be made to pay.'

Her lips tightened. She nodded, her eyes distant.

Bellard was watching her. 'You said there's a story you don't understand, yet you don't seem surprised he's ended up in jail.'

'Actually, I'm shocked, trying to work out what's happened. He was riding to town to tell you that his brother has been kidnapped by dangerous men.'

'Which happens to be the story he told me, but I don't see where you fit into all this.'

'I met him yesterday. I need his help.'

'Met him?' Bellard managed to look sceptical. 'You're a stranger in Nathan's Ford, Lil. Are you saying you came a-looking for him? And if so, from where?'

'All the way from Wasteland, on the other side of the Big Bend Desert,' she said. 'A man called Blackjack Chancer has moved into premises in Wasteland I used to run as a hotel. He's turned it into a gambling Eldorado. I want it back.'

Travis cleared his throat. He'd been standing close to Bellard, but moved away so that the sunlight slanting through the window touched his high cheekbones and the intelligent grey eyes.

'What makes you believe Lukus can help?'

Choosing her words carefully, Lil Lavender said, 'His youngest brother was brutally murdered in Chancer's place.'

'How do you know that?'

'I was there that night the kid died. I

saw everything.'

'Surely not a suitable place for a lady?' Bellard said.

'I wanted to see what Chancer had done to my hotel. Seeing what Chancer did to his brother suggests Lukus might relish the chance to bring that gambling man down a peg or two.'

Bellard laughed shortly. 'He's already done that, and it's put him in jail. Lukus Rheingold can't help you. He'll have a hard enough time climbing out of the hole he's dug for himself.'

'Maybe I can help him,' Will Travis said. Bellard shot him a glance.

'That's fine lawyer-speak, but you're jumping the gun without having all the facts. Lukus is guilty of this particular crime, and possibly a lot more besides.'

Travis raised an eyebrow. 'So what am I missing?'

Bellard shrugged. 'As a lawman I hear things, read things that land on my desk. Lukus Rheingold was a hot-blooded youngster when he left home. Rumour has it, backed up some by paperwork, that he chose the wrong way of working off all that energy.'

'Riding with a bad bunch? The owlhoot trail?'

Bellard shook his head. 'He worked on his own, a lone bandit. Always under an assumed name.'

'Oh, come on, Frank,' Travis protested. 'If that's the case you can't even be sure you're talking about the same man.'

Now Bellard cracked a smile. 'You'll find this hard to believe — I know I did — but when he walked into my office I was, at that very minute, reading about his exploits. A fading newspaper led me to old Wanted dodgers . . . ' He tailed off, spreading his hands.

'What you mean is you were reading about the exploits of a man whose name doesn't match Lukus's,' Travis said. He shook his head dismissively.

'If you have got the right man, and he's as hard and sinful as you suggest,' Lil Lavender said, 'then for the job I want done I've chosen well.'

'That's between you and him,' Will Travis said, 'if and when he gets out of jail. I've some work to do here. I'll look in to the jail this evening, see what can be done for him.'

'You do, you'll need to talk to Dave,' Bellard said. 'My wife's sick so I'm heading for home.' He glanced at Lil. 'If you want some advice, you'll do the same.'

'What, on that ornery Rheingold mule?' Then she smiled sweetly.

'Wouldn't that make me a horse-thief?'

'Go and see Bud down at the livery,' Bellard said. 'He's sure to have a mount you can buy or hire. Forget Rheingold. He's staying put.'

With a nod and a touch of the finger to his hat brim the marshal walked out of the office and down the street to collect his horse.

Lil pulled a face. 'I guess that's the end of that. I was relying on Lukus. Not sure now where I should turn.'

'Maybe I have the answer,' Travis said

carefully. 'I don't know what you've been up to, but you've been hurt, and you look bone weary. Take my advice, go back to your room in the hotel and turn in, get some sleep.'

Lil was up out of the swivel-chair, testing her legs. She paused, cocked an eyebrow.

'My hotel room? You don't miss much, do you?'

'Very little escapes my notice.'

'Lawyers always did have a reputation for being nosy sons of bitches,' she said, and her look dared him to argue.

'Go get some sleep, Lil.'

'Now why do I get the feeling you're up to no good?' She brushed past him on the way to the door, her lips pursed.

'Kindred spirits, perhaps?' He shook his head, waved her away. 'On my way down to the jail I'll see Bud Jennings about that horse you need. I'll tie it to the rail outside the hotel, get someone to give you a call.'

'And again I ask myself: is this a good man being kind, or a wicked man pulling the wool over an old lady's eyes?' she said.

Then, with a shrug of her elegant shoulders she walked out into the afternoon sunshine.

Through the open door Travis watched her cross the street at an angle, the weariness clearly evident in her walk. Then he took a flat bottle from a desk drawer, and poured himself a stiff drink.

Holding it, he dropped into the swivel-chair, still warm from the woman. He smiled absently, drank, placed the glass down, thought about Lil Lavender and the story of a hotel that Blackjack Chancer had taken from her in Wasteland.

Travis knew from the itinerant nature of some of his business that the premises Chancer moved into had once been a sleazy rooming house with pretensions. What was worrying was that he doubted if it had ever been owned by Lil Lavender. And what was with that name, for God's sake? Travis had questioned enough shady business-men to recognize falsehoods, and that name sounded as if it had been plucked out of one of her hats. Was she, like Lukus Rheingold in the all too recent past, hiding behind a false name to distance herself from wickedness?

It was Travis's firm conviction that the person calling herself Lil Lavender had, without batting an eye, sat in his office and lied through her teeth. Ah, mixed metaphors, the lawyer thought, grinning. He sipped his drink, and let his thoughts drift to Lukus Rheingold.

Marshal Frank Bellard reckoned Rheingold was as guilty as hell, and defending him would be a waste of Travis's time. Travis, on the other hand, had always worked with the clear belief that there was more than one way of skinning a cat. If defending Lukus Rheingold could only end in failure, then the man must never come before a jury.

Which brought him full tilt up against the notion that had sprung from nowhere and become more attractive as the afternoon wore on. Will Travis sipped his whiskey with great satisfaction. Through half-closed eyes he observed the small office which had from day to day become ever more suffocating, basking in unfamiliar excitement that was like the freshening breeze that reinvigorates a man at the end of a long, hot summer.

* * *

It was full dark when Will Travis left his office. Before he did so he went into a small back room and, acting mostly by feel, located his gunbelt and strapped it around his waist. The holster held a Colt .45, oiled the previous week, but last used ten years ago to blow the head off a rattlesnake. Each of the gunbelt's leather loops held a shiny brass shell. The gun's cylinder held six more.

Locking the door behind him, Travis glanced across the street to the hotel. He knew Lil Lavender's room was first-floor front, and the window was in darkness. Still asleep, or had she acquired a horse for herself and left town? Truly, he didn't care either way, for the task that lay ahead of him required his full attention. So it was on these thoughts that he concentrated as he walked unhurriedly down the street to the jail: on the possibility of failure and its long-term ramifications; on the certainty within him that he would succeed in his endeavour, and on the realization that he had made no plans for what might follow.

What Will Travis didn't know was that the thoughts filling his mind were all wasted: he was already several hours too late.

11

When Lil Lavender left Will Travis's office she knew that the door remained open. She had continued on her way across the street in the direction of the hotel until she judged that she was out of the lawyer's line of sight.

Then, dropping the convenient guise of weariness like a snake shedding its skin, she changed direction and walked rapidly down the plank walk towards the jail.

Businesses were closing. Proprietors were shutting and locking doors. Riders were heading out of town to homes, ranches. A couple of lumbering wagons creaked and rattled down the gentle slope towards the nearby river crossing that would take them into Mexico.

Lil had almost reached the jail when Marshal Frank Bellard strode out of the building, untied his horse and cantered up the street through the dust kicked up by the wagons' mule teams. He saw her, saw the direction she was taking, and frowned. But clearly his thoughts were with his wife. He continued on his way.

Lil took a deep and unexpectedly shaky breath. She had a story ready for the man Bellard had left in charge, but if he had the brains he was born with it was unlikely to fool him for long. So, for that eventuality . . . biting her lip, Lil thrust a hand into the pocket of her black jacket and felt the reassuring weight and steely chill of the object it contained. Then she mounted the steps to the jail office.

A big man was seated behind the desk, a deputy's badge on his well-worn vest. Older than Liz had expected — and therefore wiser — he had dark hair with a touch of grey. Soft brown eyes, one eyebrow raised enquiringly. He tried a smile, then winced and put a hand to a badly swollen jaw.

'You must be Smoky Willis,' Lil said.

'I believe you're holding Lukus Rheingold in one of your cells?'

'Yes, ma'am, we are.'

'Then would you please grab your keys, unlock his cell and release him into my care.'

The look in the brown eyes changed, became wary.

'And you are?'

'Lil Lavender.'

'On official business?'

'I'm sure you're acquainted with Will Travis?'

'He's a good friend, and a capable lawyer.'

'Well, you are probably aware that Marshal Bellard has been to see him. I was present. It seems there are questions about the evidence linking Rheingold to the robbery in Wasteland. Legally, there's not enough to hold him.'

'What about you? How do I know you're . . . what, exactly? Are you a lawyer? A legal representative of some obscure kind?'

Intelligent questions. Feeling any advantage her impulsive cock-and-bull story might have given her slipping away, Lil braced herself mentally.

'Neither of those,' she said, 'but I do have solid credentials.'

'Ma'am, I need to see them before I unlock that cell.'

With the merest rustle of cloth, Lil brought her hand out of her pocket and pointed the deadly little derringer pistol at the deputy's face.

'It's cocked,' she said. 'Two barrels. A bullet for each of your beautiful eyes.'

Now the brown eyes had lost all expression. The big deputy's thoughts were hidden, but Lil was reading him like an open book. He was weighing up the odds. Wondering if she had the nerve to shoot a man in cold blood; whether he could reach his pistol, draw and fire before she pulled the trigger; whether he could kill a woman. He knew the talk of planting a bullet in each eye was meant to scare him, knew also that even if she missed the target she might not kill him but she'd make a mess of his face. And his position was all wrong. The way he was sitting, his holster was below desk level, the swivel-chair had arms that would hinder any attempt at a fast draw.

'I'm waiting,' Lil said. 'And counting.'

'To three?'

Lil's smile was chilling. 'If you don't come up with that key, you'll never know, will you?'

The deputy sighed. The chair's wooden under-carriage creaked as he stood up. Deliberately he nudged the chair with his thigh and it began to roll away from him. He grabbed for the back, ostensibly to hold it still. But now the angle of his body blocked Lil's view of his right hand. Smoothly, he dipped a hand to his holster and swung to face her.

He never made the draw.

The snap the little derringer made was no louder than a dry twig crackling underfoot. But suddenly there was a slash of bright red blood across the deputy's cheekbone, and with a harsh cry he slapped a hand to his face. The shock knocked him off balance. His feet tangled with the swivel-chair's three legs. He fell backwards across the desk. His head hit an ashtray fashioned from a steer's hoof. His hat fell off. Winded, blood streaming down his face, he grabbed instinctively for the dislodged headgear. As he did so, Lil stepped smartly forward, snatched his six-gun from its holster and was away out of reach before he could react.

'With this big pistol I don't even need to aim,' Lil said, pocketing the tiny derringer. 'That scratch isn't going to kill you, so lead the way to that cell we were discussing, Smoky — and no tricks.'

The big deputy regained his feet, and glowered.

'That shot will have been heard. You'll run out of time.'

'Which is what you're playing for, and I'm not having it. Move, now.

Marshal Bellard has gone home, and even responsible citizens tend to steer well clear of trouble.'

Deliberately, Lil cocked the big pistol. The instantly recognizable, oily metallic click seemed to fill the office with an electric charge that put nerves on edge.

With one final, furious glance at the elegant woman holding him at bay with his own Colt .45, the deputy snatched a key ring from a high wooden peg on the wall behind the desk. He turned away. As he did so, Lil took a quick step forward and hit him across the base of his skull with the six-gun's barrel. The crack was like a cleaver biting into a chopping block. He went down on his knees without a sound, then sat back on his heels. His head was bowed. More blood, this fresh flow trickling from the short hair at the nape of his neck. He reached up a hand, felt the liquid warmth, made a soft exclamation of disgust.

'You're a hard man, Smoky. That

should have put you out.'

'Cold-cocked by an old woman,' he said huskily. 'I'll be laughed out of town.' Still with his back to her, he said, 'There's a vicious streak in you, ma'am. I wonder what that's got to do with Lukus Rheingold?'

'I've had enough of men stealing the bread out of my mouth, then telling me what to do. Lukus will help me put an end to some of that.'

'Willingly?'

'That's really not your concern. Now, up on your feet and let's use those keys.'

Willis was shaky when he rose, but Lil treated him with considerable caution. She stayed well back as he led the way from the office through to the adjoining cells. In that bare annexe to the main building the late-afternoon sun was shafting through high barred windows, creating patterns across the earth floor. There was a smell of disinfectant and cigarette smoke.

Only one cell was occupied. Lukus

Rheingold was sitting on the hard iron cot. He showed no emotion as the deputy appeared, blood streaming down his face, the back of his shirt glistening red. Lil's attack on Willis had been carefully calculated. It was intended to subdue the big deputy and, for the listening prisoner in his lonely cell, to be an object lesson in the cruelty Lil was prepared to inflict to achieve her goal.

Now, no words were required. The keys jangled as Willis selected one and unlocked the door to Rheingold's cell. He pulled the door open at last, then looked back in a thoughtful, absent-minded way at Lavender standing well clear with his big six-gun levelled. Then he jerked his head at Rheingold.

Lukus came off the cot in one smooth, lithe movement. He stood, flexed the fingers of his right hand, then moved to the door.

'If that's the hand you hit him with,' Lil said, 'are you going to have trouble handling a gun?'

'Only one way to find out,' Lukus said.

He came past Willis, turned and used both hands to push him bodily into the cell, then smoothly swept the six-gun from Lil's hand. Keeping it trained on the deputy he lowered the hammer with his thumb, snapped it back again, lowered it, cocked the weapon one last time and nodded his satisfaction.

'It'll do.'

'Good. The keys are in the lock. Use them. When we're back on the street, throw them into some dark alley.'

'First, there's something we need to do. I'll keep him covered. I think you'll find handcuffs in one of the desk drawers.'

'Why handcuff a man we're going to lock in a cell?'

'Because there's no point locking him in the cell if he's free to yell his head off. So we're going to gag him, and to stop him removing the gag — '

'Handcuffs.'

Lil nodded, and walked back into the

office. Both men listened in silence to her opening drawers, slamming them, trying again. Then metal clinked. When Lil returned, a pair of metal cuffs dangled from one hand and in the other she held a filthy rag.

'I think this is the cloth they use for the annual office-dusting and floor-swabbing.' She held it up. Then, revealing unexpected strength in her slender fingers, she tore off a thin strip.

'It means getting close to Willis,' Rheingold said. 'It's best if you do that.'

'Hold these,' she said, and tossed the handcuffs to Rheingold.

'You're not putting that in my mouth,' Willis said.

'Oh, but I am, my dear,' Lil said, walking into the cell. 'Sit down on the cot, Smoky. And, bearing in mind that you have a seriously bruised jaw, open up like a good boy and this'll be over before you know it.'

Keeping her body out the possible line of fire, she swiftly forced the filthy rag into the deputy's mouth. She wadded it thickly, caused a lot of pain. He winced. There was fury in his narrowed eyes. Lil then used the thin strip she'd torn from the cloth to bind the gag securely in place. She tied the knot at the back of his neck, her fingers slick with his blood. Then, calling for the cuffs, she shackled his hands behind his back.

After that they moved fast. Lil came out of the cell, Lukus clanged the door to and locked it, and they left the shackled and gagged deputy sitting on the cot as the last of the day's light was struggling through the high barred windows. Back in the office, Lukus found his gunbelt hanging on a peg, checked the six-gun for loads and buckled the belt around his waist. He tossed the bunch of keys to Lil. She opened a drawer, buried them deep under papers brown with age. Then Lukus followed her out on to the plank walk, where they stood for a moment.

The town was almost deserted. Oil lamps had been lit in the saloon,

146

seductive beacons luring men with parched throats. The few businessmen who were still about were locking up and hurrying home. They didn't give Lukus and Lil a second glance.

Lukus's horse was still at the hitch rail. With Lil beside him he walked it over to the livery barn. It took less than ten minutes for Lil to do a deal with hostler Jennings for an excellent chestnut mare. Five minutes later they were mounted and putting the somnolent town of Nathan's Ford behind them.

Ahead lay . . . what, exactly?

Lukus asked the question silently of himself as he rode into the warm evening breeze; the answer came unbidden and with foreboding: they were, he realized, a mismatched pair, and they were riding into the unknown. Lil Lavender's threat still hung over his head, because he had not got rid of the stolen cash. But he was riding to Wasteland to find Kris. If he was successful, he would make Chancer pay for whatever he had done to Kris that had left the family home spattered with fresh blood.

It was quite likely that in the course of those events, Lil Lavender would get her hotel back from the Wasteland gambler.

That would be a bonus. What should be done with the stolen money was of little consequence, and could be dealt with later.

12

They did some clearing-up in the wrecked living room, followed that with a light fried meal, then walked out on to a gallery lit by a sprinkling of stars and a pale rising moon. Lil sat in the creaking rocking-chair she seemed to have claimed as her own, lit one of her thin cigars and was soon shrouded in thin blue smoke. Lukus leaned against the balcony rail, lost in thought.

He was a hard man, and on the owlhoot trail he had won through in countless violent confrontations with men who were as tough as him with both fists and guns. But those were situations in which, if he was the loser, the hurt would affect nobody but himself. Now everything had changed. His concern was not for himself — if that had ever been the case — but for his remaining brother.

Blackjack Chancer was holding a badly beaten Kris. The gambler wanted his money returned, and it was doubtful if he was a man renowned for his patience. Though there could be no certainty about it, if Lukus was going to find his brother, Wasteland was the obvious place to start the hunt. Also, Chancer's Wasteland Eldorado was Lil Lavender's former hotel. With a faint smile, Lukus decided he liked the idea of killing two birds with one stone.

'You planning on staying here the night?' Lil said. 'Risky, don't you think? You must know Bellard will come after you.'

'After both of us.' Lukus shrugged. 'The way I feel now, let him come.'

'Doesn't that mean my valiant efforts to get you out of jail were in vain?'

'What you did to Willis was vicious, not valiant, and you made sure I could hear. Was that your idea of intimidation? By then you must have known

Kris comes first, and to hell with your threat of jail.'

She rocked the creaking chair, blew a thin stream of smoke, followed it with her eyes as it drifted to veil her view of the moon.

'Got a fine aroma, and it keeps the mosquitoes away,' she said, as if feeling Lukus's gaze. 'Helps me think, too — though I'm not getting anywhere. I thought I'd got a hard man dancing to my tune, but now it's Blackjack Chancer sawing away at his fiddle.'

'To get your hotel back would need an army,' Lukus said, 'not a lone foot soldier with other worries on his mind.'

'For an army we need recruits,' Lil said, and when she turned to Lukus she nodded towards the moonlit trail. 'If you listen hard you'll hear the first of them heading this way.'

'I'm listening. Heard those hoofbeats a while before you did.'

Deliberately he kept his back turned to the sounds, though his heartbeat began to quicken uncomfortably as the pounding hoofbeats drew closer. 'You saying this is not Bellard and his deputy?'

She didn't answer and he went on, 'You look smug. Is there something you're not telling me?'

'While you were taking your ease in Bellard's jail I spent some time in Will Travis's office. He's uncomfortable in his profession, shocked to hear you were in jail and intrigued by what the marshal told him about your past.'

'What Bellard told him came off Wanted dodgers so brown and faded a man wouldn't recognize the picture if the outlaw was his own mother.'

Now Lukus did turn as the hoofbeats swelled to a thunderous pounding that was an assault on the ears. Then the approaching horse seemed to explode out of the trees lining the trail. It was moving at full gallop, its lathered flanks glistening in the moonlight. Travis, stretched along its neck, brought it clear up to the house without slackening pace.

There he sat hard back in the saddle and hauled on the reins hard enough to snap leather. The horse reared, dropped back on its haunches. Then it stamped its front hoofs down and, standing stiff-legged and quivering, snorted its indignation. But by then Travis was down and jogging. Without bothering to tie the reins, he ignored the steps and leaped on to the gallery.

'You lost your goddam senses?' he said angrily. 'Bellard's not a man to let the grass grow. He can't be more than a half-hour behind me — '

'With a posse?'

'No, dammit.' Travis shook his head. 'I told you: he won't waste time, and he's a man confident of his own capabilities. You need to move fast. Where are your horses?'

'In the corral, but — '

'Then get out of here.'

'To Wasteland?'

'Not Wasteland,' Lil said, and the rocking-chair creaked furiously as she came gracefully to her feet. 'For that we need some preparation. We move out now, but only far enough to make him believe he's already too late.'

Travis gestured. 'There's a stand of trees behind the house.'

'Shelter for my family's graves,' Lukus said, and he nodded agreement as he saw the good sense in the idea. 'Thick woods are always difficult to search in the dark. If there're graves in the area, superstition makes most men wait for first light.'

Travis had gone to the gallery's rail and was looking hard into the night as he listened to sounds all three of them could hear clearly.

'Go,' Travis said.

Taking hold of Lil Lavender's arm, Lukus lead her quickly through the house to the back door and across the moonlit yard to the corral. Then they walked their horses across the coarse grass to the slope leading up to the knoll where moonlight filtered through dark pines to faintly illuminate three wooden crosses.

'You look thoughtful, Will.'

Frank Bellard was sitting in the rocking-chair so recently warmed by Lil Lavender. Will Travis had come out of the house with two steaming cups of coffee, and was leaning against the rail.

'I knew what to expect when I rode out here,' he said. 'Lukus and the woman were long gone. If I'm to help him, I've some tough riding to do.'

'A little bird told me you walked into my jail, walked right out again. Who told you it was Lavender let him out?'

'Her manner when she walked out of my office.' Travis crossed the gallery and sat down on the boards with his back against the still-warm house wall. 'I thought: she'll wait until dark, but she got in early, saved me from committing a criminal act.'

'Is that a fact?' Bellard turned to look at him, shook his head in disbelief. 'Well, don't really matter who opened the cell door and locked up Smoky

Willis. If you're right, by now Lukus and that hotel-keeper turned jail-breaker are leaving cattle country and heading into the desert.'

He paused, taking his time. 'You watched me ride around the house, Will. That was the act of an old lawman wise to man's perfidy; even an honest lawyer can make a fairy tale sound like truth. So I took a look around. Out back the moon was picking out the crosses marking the Rheingold graves in the woods: Lukus's ma and pa, and young Christian. More telling was that the only live critter in the corral is that stubborn old mule. No horses, so, yes, they're gone, and I had it all figured out without you telling me.'

'If you thought it through you could have saved yourself a ride.'

'Another thing a wise lawman does is leave nothing to chance,' Bellard said as if quoting from a book, and he grinned. 'You're dressed like a backwoodsman, Will. Got a six-gun strapped on under that worn old buckskin, and there's a rifle out there in your saddle boot. Forget to shave for a couple of days, grow whiskers and throw a couple of fresh deer hides across your saddle . . . '

He sipped his drink, shook his head. 'I'll get word to Wasteland. Take a while, because there's no telegraph here or there. But they'll be a good few days crossing the desert, time for that Wasteland marshal Jed Crane to have a hot reception waiting when they ride in.'

'When I catch up with them, I'll pass on the warning.'

'Ain't no 'when' in it. You're going nowhere.'

'There's nothing you can do to stop me leaving.'

'Short of arresting you, you mean? Well, that's easy done.'

'On what charge?'

'How about we say Lil Lavender was acting on your orders? Speaking as a lawyer, what's the term for that? Accessory? And then there's the bit they add on, before or after the fact, which always leaves me puzzled.'

Will Travis laughed at Bellard's easy rambling. He leaned his head back, then reached up and ran both hands through his hair. The action caused his buckskin coat to fall open, either by accident or intent. It left the butt of his six-gun exposed.

Watching him from the rocking-chair, Bellard again shook his head.

'I don't know if that's a threatening move, or not,' he said, 'but it doesn't really matter. I was just exercising my lungs, Will, I'm not arresting you. And I'm not stopping you leaving. As for catching up with Lukus and the woman, well, that shouldn't take you too long.'

'By my reckoning,' Travis said, 'they have a good two hours' start.'

'They may have set out two hours ago, but they got no further than those woods out back.' Bellard smiled sadly. 'Rheingold may be a tough nut, but he's gone stale an' taken to underestimating the opposition. Maybe he didn't expect me there, nosing around behind the house. He got restless and lit a cigarette, and that was mighty careless.'

'If you know he's out there, what now?'

'Now nothing,' Bellard said, and he heaved himself out of the chair, held it with his hand to still its rocking. 'I told you once I leave nothing to chance, and right now I don't like the odds. Besides, I know where Rheingold's going, so I guess you can say I'll live to fight another day.'

He walked away and off the gallery, knowing Travis was watching him and wondering. *Well, let him wonder,* Bellard thought. He swung into the saddle and set off down the trail without a backward glance.

Half a mile out, in an area where trees blocked any view from the house, a scummed pool gleamed a moonlit green in a hollow and there was an overpowering stench of rotting horse-flesh. A rider came out to meet him. A big man with a shiny badge on his vest.

A man with an open gash on his face, who, when he spoke, was very careful in the way he moved his jaw.

'They're still there, all of 'em,' Bellard said, drawing rein.

'You and me, we could take them,' Smoky Willis said. 'Why wait?'

'Because of Kris Rheingold. I believe the story I was told, but why should we go looking for Kris when we know Chancer has him in Wasteland? Lukus and Will Travis will sort things out one way or another. I don't know where that woman fits in all of this, but that's a concern for later.'

'The robbery was committed by the Rheingold's in Wasteland,' Willis pointed out, 'the jailbreak here by Lil Lavender. And now they've got Will Travis hangin' on to their shirt tails, and he's a lawyer.'

'Yeah, I told him, that's an attorney, aiding and abetting,' Bellard said, grinning. 'I don't know where, or when, but chances are all three of 'em — four if Kris is still alive — are heading for a spell in the calaboose.'

'There's something else you should know,' Willis said.

'Go on.'

'Lavender used a derringer on me — that was before she cold-cocked me with my own six-gun. Point is, being handcuffed, gagged and locked in a cell gives a man time to think. Her using that little derringer was the trigger,' — the listening marshal chuckled — 'and after that it was easy. I've seen her before, Frank, some ways from here but not in Wasteland. Dressed up to the nines, she looked too damn highfalutin to be an old maid running a posh rooming house.' He paused. 'An old feller pointed her out to me. He said, 'That there is Diamond Lil Malone,' and I swear to God that man had gone pale in the face.'

PART THREE

13

Kris Rheingold was on his knees. It was early morning. He was kneeling on damp gravel. He gasped, shuddering with pain as he splashed the ice-cold water of the Rio Grande over his battered face, his broken nose. When he cautiously shook the droplets from his wet hair and looked out over the glittering ribbon of river, he saw everything through his right eye. His left was swollen shut. Planting his hands in the water, he struggled awkwardly to his feet. Dizziness washed over him and he staggered sideways. Wet gravel crunched beneath his boots. His crippled right leg buckled and he almost fell. Fighting for balance, he heard a chilling laugh. Then a vicious kick delivered by the gunslinger Fallon took his legs from under him and he fell, twisting backwards into the river.

Even that close to the bank the water was deep. Kris went under, came up spluttering. He thrashed his arms, tried to kick with his feet and realized his mistake: the rawhide strip linking his ankles in a crude hobble snapped tight, the wet leather biting into his flesh. Again he went under, felt the gravel sliding away under his shoulders, the current pulling him ever deeper.

Deprived of oxygen, gazing almost dreamily up at the glittering sunlit surface of the river and feeling the will to live seeping away like blood from an open wound, he was suddenly jerked to a halt. A hand had grasped the linking strip of rawhide. Again the leather bit into his ankles. Opening his mouth to yell, 'Dammit, no, leave me be,' he sucked ice-cold water into his lungs, and choked. Coughing, retching, spewing up mud and mucus and seeing life through a red haze, he was dragged feet first out of the river.

He turned over and was on his belly, flat out, face against the wet stones. His breathing settled. His heart stopped hammering.

Wearily, huskily, he said, 'Is there a point to all this?'

'Money's part of it,' Fallon said. 'The cash you stole from Chancer. Tell me where it is, this is over, finished.'

'Yeah, I'll bet it is,' Kris said, and again he rolled, fought his way to his knees, to his feet, stood panting. 'I tell you where Chancer's money's hidden, I'm a dead man. You'll put a slug in me, or get your friend up there to use a knife.' He gestured to the Mexican, sitting outside the ruined adobe, impassively smoking a cigarette. 'Then you take the good news to Chancer, and that's the end of my brother. And that's why, no matter what you do, you'll get nothing out of me.'

'Most men I deal with,' Fallon said, 'end up talking.'

'I'm talking now, talking plain, and talking truthful. Do your worst, Fallon,' Kris said.

'You know about Laredo?'

'What?'

'Your brother tell you what he did down there? Few years back? Because if he did you'll know I meant what I said, that money's a reason for what's happening, but not the only one. Hell, if you get to do some deep thinking, you'll begin to understand that Chancer's money's the least of your worries.'

'I don't know what the hell you're talking about,' Kris said. He turned away from the gunslinger and began hobbling up the grassy bank.

He heard Fallon whistling softly through his teeth. Waited for the kick that would again bring him to his knees. It didn't come. There was a musical plink, plink, plink, and he knew that for the moment Fallon had forgotten him. He had gone to the water's edge, and was amusing himself by skimming flat stones.

Trouble was, Kris had been bluffing. He knew exactly what Fallon was talking about. Lukus had returned home six months ago, and in the first few days he'd talked non-stop. On the gallery. Over breakfast. In town bellied up against the bar. Baring his soul, he'd called it — and that baring had included confession, about a man he'd killed while seconded to the Texas Rangers. But that man, Kris recalled, had been called Kane, and he wondered why a dead man called Kane would be so important to another man called Fallon.

In the shade under the grey-green cottonwoods that sheltered the walls that were all that remained of the adobe dwelling, Kris sank down on to a log. The Mexican ignored him. Unshaven, wearing a ragged and faded sombrero, he was sitting cross-legged, leaning back against what was left of the adobe's walls and gazing out across the river through the veil of cigarette smoke.

He can see what I can see, Kris thought, and he wondered how much the Mexican knew. Did he know that the ranch buildings across the water, close to the west bank of the river, belonged to a man called Cage and the woman Violet Goodwine? Did he know that, a couple of years ago, Cage was almost killed in a gunfight with Mexican bandits in and around the ruined walls against which he was leaning? Somehow he'd made his way across the river as a rain of bullets ripped up the water. Had staggered up the bank a bloodstained ruin of a man, to be faced by another *loco* Mexican holding a pistol to Violet Goodwine's head.

Maybe he does know all of that, Kris thought. Maybe that gunfight was still talked about over mescal drunk under flickering oil lamps in his pueblo's smoky cantina. But what the Mexican couldn't know was that, for some time, Kris had seen a glimmer of hope and had been racking his brain looking for a way of communicating with the man called Cage. Or that, as he hobbled up the bank with the heat of the sun on his back, a vivid picture had flashed into his mind, almost bringing him to a halt: a picture of soldiers on a barren hillside where dead bodies lay, signalling to their colleagues over a great distance by such a simple means as the sun's reflection.

Cage and the V Slash C ranch were no great distance away. Just a river's width. And, much earlier that morning, Kris Rheingold had painfully examined his battered countenance, using for a mirror a bit of shiny tin flattened from an empty sardine can. In west Texas and this part of Mexico, most days were blessed with bright sunlight from dawn to dusk.

Seated on his log, prepared to accept the pain he knew it would cause, Kris Rheingold cracked a broad grin. Heliograph, that was the name of that dang thing soldiers used for signalling. And, dammit, didn't he have one right there in his pocket?

14

The crossing of the Big Bend Desert was taken slowly: a couple of days to cover the fifty-odd miles. Neither Lukus Rheingold nor Lil Lavender were strangers to the searing heat, the thirst that seemed impossible to slake. Lil had made the most recent crossing, arriving in Nathan's Ford just a couple of days ago. Lukus had made the crossing four times, each time accompanied by Kris.

Will Travis, dressed for the part, as the Nathan's Ford marshal had noted, took the crossing stoically, his lean, mustachioed countenance grey with dust but his sharp eyes for much of the time gleaming with an inner satisfaction that was close to excitement.

They had left the Rheingold spread at dawn, carrying with them water and food, and enough ammunition for all their weapons — excluding, Lukus had said, Lil Lavender's toy pistol. She had brushed aside his contempt for, packed away in the saddle-bags that came with the horse sold to her by Nathan's Ford's hostler, she had spare shells for the gambler's pistol, and Smoky Willis's loaded six-gun.

Lukus insisted on taking the mule to lighten the load on the horses. All supplies were carried by the black, gawky animal with the pointed ears and awkward temperament. Lukus's decision was justified, but his explanation fell some way short of the truth. He had work for the stubborn animal, work to which it was accustomed.

Just after dawn on the third day the landscape changed. From the seemingly endless flat expanse of sand, rocks and parched scrub under cruel white skies they rode into a fertile region, where tall grass was blown into green waves by cooling breezes and cottonwoods lined fast-flowing creeks that sparkled as a friendlier sun climbed above the horizon.

They dismounted at the first clear water and swilled their faces. Then Lukus led them to No End Creek. It was here that his insistence on bringing the mule was explained.

'What I see ahead of us,' Will Travis said, 'must be the Rheingold buckboard Frank Bellard told me you and Kris put into the river.'

'I'm surprised nobody's claimed it as their own,' Lukus said. 'That was bothering me some.'

'Bothering you,' Travis said, 'because clearly you have a use for it.'

'Of course he has,' Lil Lavender told Travis, 'and it's not hard to figure. The three of us riding into Wasteland like bandits would be asking for trouble. A buckboard paints a different picture.'

While talking they'd ridden under the trees overhanging the narrow, sloping trail and drawn level with the buckboard. It was as steeply canted as Lukus remembered, and he recalled it shifting on the rocks as he and Kris struggled to get the mule out of the traces. Thoughts of his brother tightened Lukus's jaw. He slid out of the saddle, put his hands on the buckboard side boards. The coffin was where they had left it; open, and stinking. The vultures had been at the dead sheep. What was left was mostly bones.

'So what's your plan?' Will Travis said, bringing his horse close in and peering into the wagon. 'Getting rid of that foul mess is easy enough, and with three horses and a mule we'll have no trouble dragging the wagon out of the creek. But then what?'

'We hitch the mule in the traces,' Lukus said.

'What's that going to achieve?'

'We all climb aboard and head for town,' Lil said. 'It's a battle wagon.'

'No.' Lukus shook his head. 'You take the wagon into town, Will, on your own. Chancer doesn't know you, and without the dead sheep the buckboard looks like any other old farm cart. Take it round the back of the building. His office is there, and he'll be busy doing what he likes best, counting his money. You're a lawyer, well able to think up a plausible story. That will hold Chancer and Fallon long enough for me to make my way through the building.'

'And take 'em from the rear.' Travis nodded approval. 'The building was Lil's hotel, so she knows it well. Do you want her with you?'

'I don't think he does,' Lil said. 'Anyway, though it's been fitted up for gambling it's still mostly just one big room. The night I was in there I was watching Chancer. He was in and out the door at the far end. That has to be the back way into his office.'

'Then that's all we need to know,' Lukus said. 'I'll bust a way into the main building through the door or a window.'

'What about me?'

'Go home, Lil.'

She hesitated for a moment, then shrugged. 'You know, I think that's exactly what I'll do. I had you over a barrel, Lukus, but I know any threat died the death when your brother was taken. You're going to take on Chancer with or without my gentle persuasion. The result could be good for both of us.'

Lukus's smile was cynical. 'A lot of truth in there, but my real reason for wanting you gone is because you'll be the second . . . decoy . . . diversion, whatever you want to call it. Will's going to keep them occupied by going in the back way. I'll ride in tight against the buildings adjoining the Eldorado. If Fallon does happen to be watching — maybe sent upstairs by Chancer to keep an eye out for trouble — all he'll see is you riding across that big street to your rooming house.'

'With that settled,' Will Travis said, 'there's only one thing left for us to do.'

'Right,' Lukus agreed. 'Let's get the mule hitched, and drag this buckboard out of the creek.'

15

The sun was nowhere near its zenith: this worked favourably for Lukus Rheingold. Ten minutes after Will Travis trundled the Rheingold buckboard across Wasteland's main street and up the wide alley between the Eldorado and the adjoining premises, Lukus brought his roan in along the plank walk and the front of those buildings and found himself in deep shadow.

There he paused.

Travis had brought the buckboard in along the recognized trail. But there were others, some little more than tracks through the grass worn over the years by the passage of wild animals heading for water holes. Lil Lavender had taken her hired mount to the north, then used one of those snaking trails to enter town. Now, from his vantage point in the shade of those business premises, Lukus watched her.

Her approach was unhurried. She took the horse across the square at a walk. Halfway across the dusty expanse she let it draw to a halt. She took a kerchief from a pocket and mopped her brow. Then she lightly touched the horse with her heels and took it all the way to the line of smaller buildings on that side of the street. She pulled up in front of one with a red tin roof and a wide, shaded gallery. She tied the horse up at the rail, then stepped up on to the gallery and became a vague black figure almost lost in the shade.

Ma Foley's, Lukus read, squinting through the sunlight at the distant sign nailed to one of the gallery's uprights. And, beneath the name, *Welcome, stranger. Rooms to let. Home from home.*

His only thought — because his mind was occupied with other more dangerous matters — was that when Lil Lavender took over that rooming house she retained the original name for the goodwill.

Then, forgetting her, he flicked the reins and the big roan took him through shadows made intense by the dazzling light beating down on the dusty street. On the block before Blackjack Chancer's Eldorado he dismounted and tied his horse to a convenient rail.

He loosened his six-gun in its holster; then, still keeping as much as he could to the shadows, he went the rest of the way on foot.

Lukus found a way in through a window in a narrow alley alongside the Eldorado. No glass, just a board nailed across the opening from the inside. He took his hat off, used it to protect his fist and dull the sound. Then he punched his way in.

He climbed into a small storeroom. Dusty shelves, cardboard boxes, a stepladder, a couple of buckets. The door was unlocked. He went through like a ghost and found himself in the big room Lil had described. He was no gambler, could recognize at once only the roulette table. The rest, well, he glanced at them as he padded through the room and reckoned they must tally with the outside sign and offer keno, chuck-a-luck, poker, craps and any other game devised to fleece the suckers.

The decor was garish, mostly a rich red, a colour designed to make a man reckless while taking his mind off the life-savings he was putting in Chancer's pockets. In the faint light the only glitter was provided by the roulette wheel and the bar that took up much of one long wall.

As he made his way to the door at the far end of the room, the muffled murmur of voices came to Lukus through the oak panels. A little over a week ago he had seen Blackjack Chancer when Kris, calling himself Joe Martin, had been entertaining Jed Crane's posse on the banks of No End Creek. Chancer: a man conceited enough to believe he was larger than life when he flashed his teeth in the mirror and brushed his blond hair; a man who was about to see that image shattered for all time.

Without pause Lukus drew his six-gun and walked into the office.

'You took your time,' Blackjack Chancer said.

The big table was bare, the safe locked. There was no sign of Fallon. Will Travis was sitting cross-legged in a corner. His hands were making fists in his lap, bound with rawhide. Chancer was seated at the table. A bone-handled six-gun lay in front of him. It looked big enough to blow a hole in a longhorn steer.

'You knew I went to Nathan's Ford after we took your brother,' Chancer said. 'I went there to talk to the marshal, let him know what the Rheingold boys had been up to, get the law working on my side. Didn't it cross your mind I might have seen your lawyer friend? I did, and I recognized him as soon as he rolled up in that buckboard.' Chancer shook his head. 'Then he told me he's a lawyer, and started spouting some cock-and-bull story about abduction and taking a man against his will and — '

'Where's my brother?'

'With Fallon.'

'That tells me damn all, Chancer.'

'You'll see him again, alive, when you've emptied a sack of money on to that table. If you've got it out there, stuffed in your saddle-bags, then go fetch them and we're in business. If not, you're finished here.'

'There was enough blood splashed in my living room to suggest I won't recognize Kris when I do see him. And I will see him, Chancer, because you're going to hand him over to me with or without that money.'

Chancer sat forward, both hands on the edge of the table.

Lukus cocked his six-gun with a loud snap.

Chancer froze.

'You're a fine-looking man, Chancer,'

Lukus said. 'Just like Kris, only getting old in a hurry. Nevertheless, I say what's good for the goose is good for the gander. A pistol-whipping does a lot of damage. Livid scars on a man's face will make women who might have fallen for your charms turn their heads away with a shudder.'

'Lukus, that's not a good way to go about this,' Will Travis said huskily.

'It's not a good way or bad way, it's the only way,' Lukus said. 'Blackjack Chancer knows where Fallon's holding my brother. He's going to tell me, or he'll look like something that's come off a butcher's block — '

Then the inner door banged open.

Lukus spun. Lil Lavender stepped into the room. She was holding a shotgun. Her eyes, fixed on Blackjack Chancer, were like blue ice. She pulled back the shotgun's hammers, lifted it, levelled it at Chancer.

'Lil, no, don't,' Lukus roared. He took a fast step towards her, hand outstretched, reaching, clutching.

His hand touched her jacket. His fingers curled, began to close like claws. He tried to chop down on the shotgun with his pistol, missed, and then it was too late.

'Say goodbye, Blackjack,' Lavender said, so softly she might have been speaking to herself. Then she pulled the triggers and both barrels belched flame. In that small room the blast was like a charge of dynamite, the effect just as devastating. Chancer's white shirt front became shredded cloth, failing to cover a terrible wound out of which blood gushed. The powerful impact knocked the big man backwards. The chair went over with a splintering crash. Chancer lay still, bleeding on to the dirt floor. Will Travis, hands bound, used the strength of his legs against the wall to push himself upright. He stumbled across to the dying gambler, dropped to his knees.

Now Lukus had hold of Lil Lavender. His hand was clutching her jacket, bunching it, thrusting it up under her soft chin. The shotgun clattered to the floor. When she looked at him, her gaze was distant, her thin smile chilling. He released his hold, pushed her away from him in disgust.

'You know what you've done?' he said hoarsely.

'Everyone in the room knows what I've done, except maybe Blackjack Chancer, and he's past caring.'

'I care. Chancer's the only man who knows where Fallon is holding my brother, and dead men don't talk.'

'So find Fallon.'

Then Will Travis came over. His bound hands were red and glistening. Lukus grimaced, brought out his pocket knife and slashed the rawhide bonds.

'There's something you should know,' Travis said, wiping his hands on his pants, then massaging his wrists. 'Chancer's dead, but he got out some words along with the blood he was coughing up. He says neither he nor the men in his employ had anything to do with the death of your kid brother.'

'A negative's no damn good,' Lavender said. 'I was in that big room back there, being jostled in a crowd of excited gamblers but close enough to that craps table to get splashes of blood on my shirt. I saw nothing. The noise in there was deafening, but a shot should have been heard — '

'He was knifed,' Lukus said.

'I should have figured that. But if not by Chancer or one of his hired guns, then who's the killer?'

All three of them were standing there chewing over the big gambling man's dying words when Marshal Jed Crane and his deputy Buck Aitken charged in out of the alley with grim looks and drawn guns.

16

'The woman's no problem,' Jed Crane said. 'She's safely behind bars and likely to get her neck stretched. But what do I do about you, Rheingold?'

'Why do anything?'

'If a woman can get names from an undertaker named Martin, I sure as hell can do the same. Which I did. Then Chancer came out of the desert and gave me those same names. You and your brother.'

'Blackjack Chancer's dead. Doesn't that leave me and my brother in the clear?'

'Good point, but debatable. But if you return this cash you're supposed to have stolen,' Crane said, 'who do I hand it to?'

'Chancer's estate,' Will Travis said.

'Just supposing I'm going to the sweat of looking for his next of kin,'

Crane said, 'which I ain't.'

They were in Crane's office. Deputy Aitken had gone home to his wife. Lil Lavender was stretched out on a cot in one of the cells, covered by a thin blanket and deep in untroubled sleep. The air in the office was fogged with cigarette smoke. Lukus was slumped despondently in a straight chair. Chancer's killing, and the question of where that left his brother and the gunman Fallon, had knocked the wind out of him.

'I've a next of kin to look for and I don't know where the hell to start,' he said. 'Fallon's somewhere hereabouts . . .'

'Here?' Behind his desk with his feet up, Crane shook his head. 'Fallon's not here. A couple of us were out that way and saw Chancer come out of the desert. He was alone. You ask me, Fallon never started out from Nathan's Ford with your brother.'

Lukus swore softly, slammed a clenched fist on his knee.

'Steady now,' Travis said. 'Looking for a needle in a haystack could be easier now the haystack's been moved closer to home.'

'But if you stop folk and ask if they've seen him, heard of him,' Crane said, 'make sure you use Fallon's full name.'

'What?' Lukus was frowning.

'Fallon's the middle bit, the one he likes best. His full moniker's John Fallon Kane.'

'Jesus Christ!' Lukus breathed. 'He said he knew me. I saw a likeness, but couldn't pin it down. Now I can. Four or five years ago I killed a man in self-defence. I'd made the crossing from Laredo into Mexico. For some reason I can't recall, I was working on the side of the law. Mexican bandits were stealing cattle in Texas and swimming them across the river by moonlight.'

'Still happening,' Travis said. 'I do legal work for ranchers raising cattle around Nathan's Ford, some with big losses.'

'This was a real wild bunch; anyone

got in their way on the Texas side of the river, they'd kill them,' Lukus said. 'At the dead of night, so it was always knives. Two white men were with them. They'd spend some time riding the range on the Texas side of the river, locate a prosperous ranch ripe for the picking, take the word to their bandit *amigos*.'

'And you killed one of 'em?'

'Ed Kane.'

'Fallon's brother. But Fallon got away?'

'Clear away. It was a night operation, me and a bunch of Texas Rangers in ambush along a deep arroyo. Let the steers through, caught the bandits cold. Those we didn't cut down in the first salvo took off into the desert wilderness.'

And Fallon must have had sharp eyes and a long memory,' Will Travis said. 'You realize this changes everything? The way I saw it, if Fallon got wind of Chancer's death he'd have no more use for Kris and would let him go. That's not going to happen. Might never have happened. Chancer was using your brother as a threat so you'd hand over his cash. It's likely that once Fallon recognized you in Chancer's office he'd see this as between you and him.'

'With the cash as a bonus if he could take it for himself.' Lukus nodded. 'It also explains all that blood in my house,' he added. 'Kris took a bad beating, and now we know why.'

'There's been a lot of double-dealing muddying the waters,' Will Travis said, and rolled his eyes. 'Fallon's been playing his own game. Lil Lavender said she wanted your help getting her hotel back, but was she ever telling the truth?'

'There is no Lil Lavender,' Jed Crane said.

Will raised an eyebrow. 'Somebody's locked up back there.'

'The woman you know as Lavender is Diamond Lil Malone. If you've heard of Pine Rivers you'll know about the short-lived gambling ban. Diamond Lil ran a successful gambling joint, making her money out of stacked decks, loaded dice and a roulette wheel with a convenient brake. When the ban came into force she was out of town — a business deal of some kind. Blackjack Chancer moved in, loaded her equipment on to a fleet of buckboards and took 'em south. The building he took over here used to be a hotel, sure, but it was never Diamond Lil's.'

'Lavender or Malone, she didn't need me after all,' Lukus said. 'In the end, it was her killed Chancer.'

'Without you she wouldn't have got close,' Crane said, 'so there was a half-truth buried in her story: she needed you, but only so she could get to Chancer. And today she did that. She followed you in knowing there'd be a shotgun behind the bar, because back in Pine Rivers it was her bar, her shotgun.' Crane shrugged his powerful shoulders, grimaced at Lukus. 'So, with all that out of the way, we come back to the question I asked.'

'About me? There's a man out there using my brother the way a backwoodsman would tether a goat to trap a cougar. I'm riding back across the Big Bend to settle his hash.'

'Not unless we reach a clear understanding. There's been some banter over this stolen cash. The plain truth is it's in your possession — meaning that somewhere there's a hole in the ground you filled with something more than raw earth. You guarantee to hand that money over to me when you've settled with Fallon, and you leave here with my good wishes. You refuse, you'll be in the next cell to Diamond Lil listening to her snoring.'

For a moment, Lukus hesitated. His eyes met Crane's. He nodded slowly, thoughtfully.

'Yes, OK. You have my word.'

He turned on his heel and walked out.

Will Travis was on his feet, somehow getting his hat correctly planted while shaking his head in disbelief at the marshal.

'You trust him?'

'Can't see why not.'

'Lukus Rheingold rode the owlhoot.'

'I'm a lawman. Rheingold's history is no secret, though he likes to believe it is.' Jed Crane's smile was crooked, his eyes wise. 'The reason I took his word, let him walk out of here, is because I wasn't talking to him — I was talking to you.'

PART FOUR

PART FOUR

17

Leaving the buckboard and mule in the care of the town's hostler, they set out from Wasteland along No End Creek early in the evening on that same day. They left lush grassland behind as the hills to the north were fading behind a purple haze, entered the desolate landscape of undulating sandy wastes thinly covered with low scrub and began to push their mounts hard.

They crossed the Big Bend Desert at a relentless pace. As darkness fell, the temperature dropped. The burning heat of the desert rose in waves from the ground over which they rode, but the air's night-time chill was bearable to the riders and enabled the horses to cover mile after endless mile without noticeably slowing, or becoming unduly tired. They stopped just once for a fifteen-minute break, drinking from water bottles then splashing water into their hats for the horses.

When dawn was a sliver of light stretching clear across the horizon at their backs, the landscape changed again. Scrub became coarse grass, then rich pasture. The horses caught the scent of the Rio Grande and their gait picked up. The first rays of the rising sun were painting with gold the tall pines that sheltered the family graves when Lukus led the way on to the Rheingold spread.

'Someone's been here,' he said. He swung down in haste and stood staring at the house.

Steam was rising from horse-droppings close to the hitch rail. In the cold, still air there was the faint sharp smell of cigarette smoke. The front door of the house was open.

'We just missed him,' Will Travis said. He was also out of the saddle. He tied his horse, casting his eyes everywhere.

'Him?' Lukus said.

'Fallon.'

'If it was him,' Lukus said, 'he was after the money. He'll have searched, but found nothing.'

'You sure?'

But Lukus's thoughts were racing ahead.

'It had to be Fallon. But if it was, where's Kris?'

He'd mounted the steps while talking, and now crossed the gallery and went into the house. Again, the smell of cigarette smoke. In the dawn light filtering through door and windows it was clear that the house had been searched.

'Damn it,' Lukus said softly, and he kicked angrily at cushions that had been thrown from upholstered chairs, which had themselves been tipped over.

'We'll eat, then talk,' Will Travis said. He brushed past Lukus and made for the kitchen.

'He didn't come up the trail from town,' Travis said.

'My turn to ask if you're sure.'

'You were angry. I was using my eyes.

He came in from the west, cutting across country. The tracks where his horse came through the long grass are plain to see.'

'If you're that good,' Lukus said, 'then you'll know if he was alone.'

'He was. So if he's still holding Kris he's got him locked up somewhere, or he'll have someone standing guard.'

Breakfast was finished. Both men were on the gallery, Will sitting smoking a cigarette in the rocking-chair, Lukus leaning against the rail. The sun was already hot on his back. He thought about what Travis had said, and closed his eyes.

'What are you saying, Will?'

'Fallon doesn't give a damn about Blackjack Chancer, doesn't know he's dead,' Travis said. 'Years ago he saw you kill his brother, and that's why he took Kris. But for all he knows, Chancer could have plugged you. If you're pushing up daisies, he's stuck with a hostage who's now a liability. If you were Fallon, what would you do?'

'Cut my losses,' Lukus said at once. 'He didn't find the cash. To get even with me he can put a bullet in Kris's head.'

For a few minutes there was silence, each man lost in his thoughts. Will pushed the boards with his foot. The rocking-chair creaked.

'If we go into town,' he said, 'Bellard will throw you in jail.'

'Why would we?'

'Whatever's happened, you're going to look for Kris. Asking questions would be a start.'

'But why waste time doing that,' Lukus said, coming away from the rail, 'when there's a trail through the long grass that could lead us straight to Fallon? Then again, who the hell needs an arrow pointing the way? John Fallon Kane has crossed the river, Will. He wants a showdown with me where all those years ago one of my bullets cut a life short, and that place is Mexico.'

18

They didn't waste time.

Lukus was coldly efficient, seeing to the big roan's immediate needs, then packing the saddlebags with everything that might be needed on what he figured could be a long, tough ride. That included boxes of ammunition. Shots could be exchanged between hunter and hunted on the chase south through Mexico. Even more shells would be expended if the inevitable showdown became violent.

He told Will Travis to leave him, go back to town, work at being the town's attorney.

'That's what I'm doing,' Travis said, bending to tighten a cinch. 'I have a reckless client. He's in the habit of treading on local lawmen's corns.'

They were on their way fifteen minutes after the decision had been made. Following the trail left by Fallon — he'd used the same route in and out, Lukus noted — they rode swiftly to the Rheingold spread's western boundary and from there on to lush V Slash C pasture, where well-fed cattle grazed and there was evidence everywhere that Cage and Violet Goodwine were prospering.

A mile on to V Slash C land they heard the sound of distant rifle shots. Two faint cracks, then a third, followed by silence. Lukus and Will Travis exchanged looks, but no words were spoken. Cage's ranch house on the banks of the Rio Grande was still two miles away. They pushed on, grim-faced. In cattle-raising country there would always be an innocent explanation for rifle shots. In the circumstances, Lukus feared the worst.

The worst turned out to be a bloody mess. The gunshot victim was a Mexican lying on his back in the sloping yard leading down to the river. His clothes were saturated. He was lying in a pink pool of blood and river water. Near by, a battered sombrero was a patch of red and yellow, and a ragged bronc stood dripping.

Violet Goodwine was kneeling at the man's head. She looked up at the approaching riders, and Cage came to meet them.

'You know this involves you?' he said to Lukus.

'That's what I figured,' Lukus replied, stepping out of the saddle, 'but what happened here needs some explaining.'

He and Cage had known each other as children. Both had left town young, and returned as mature men. Since then they had spoken occasionally, usually in the Wayfarer saloon.

'There was something happening over there.' Cage gestured over his shoulder. 'We're always busy here, so I took little notice. Yesterday I was in the yard and a flash of sunlight hit me in the eye. Someone on the other side of the river was using a mirror. After that I paid more attention, but still saw nothing — '

'He's gone,' Violet Goodwine said abruptly. She stood up and came over to them, wiping the blood off her hands.

'Damn!' Cage said. The woman was almost his height. She looked shaken. Travis was still on his horse, listening. Goodwine looked at him and managed a smile.

'Did he say anything?' Lukus said to her.

It was Cage who answered. 'Some,' he said. 'He'd been shot in the back but still had breath in him when he fell off his horse. There's a feller across the river goes by the name of Fallon. He's got a prisoner. Treats him pretty bad. The Mex' — Cage gestured to the dead man — 'didn't agree with what was going on, maybe didn't understand the reasons for it.

'When Fallon's back was turned he took his chance and rode his bronc into the river. Fallon's bullets caught him when he was halfway across, and there's the result.' Cage shrugged.

'Do you understand what's going on?'

Cage nodded slowly. 'I think so, yes. I talk to Frank Bellard most days. The last time we spoke we were in his office. He had reason to mention your brother's name.'

'So you know Fallon's holding Kris?'

'That much, yes, but Bellard didn't say why.'

'There's a couple of reasons. The main one is to get back at me.'

'They set off down river when we were seeing to that poor man,' Violet Goodwine said. 'They were riding hard, and that was, oh, fifteen minutes ago?'

Cage was puzzled. 'So where the hell is he taking Kris?'

'That's something I've been thinking about,' Lukus said, swinging into the saddle and turning the big roan, 'and the answer that refuses to go away is turning my blood cold.'

★ ★ ★

'Kane couldn't find Chancer's money,' Lukus said, some time later. 'Maybe Kris was forced to tell him where it's buried, and sent him on a wild-goose chase — I don't know. But not finding it would have sent Fallon into a white-hot rage. He'd have crossed the river and turned on Kris, using fists, a club . . . I think that's what sickened the old Mex and drove him across the river to his death.'

He was talking with his head half-turned. Travis was riding a little way behind and to the side on a smaller horse. They'd realized that swimming their horses across the deeper water fronting the V Slash C would have been risky. Also, it would slow them down. The easier, quicker option was to use the shallower crossing at the town, so they were hammering back along the river towards Nathan's Ford.

'Where's he taking Kris?' Travis said, drawing closer.

'South. I think he's figuring on locating the Mexican bandits he and his brother rode with. He does that, he'll have his revenge because Kris will be gone for good. They'll take him to a village, put him to work in the fields alongside the women. Feed him scraps the dogs won't eat.'

'I'm not so sure,' the lawyer said. 'It's a long ride to Laredo. My feeling is Kane's got his mind set on that money. He won't let go.'

Lukus grunted, clamped his jaw, settled to his riding. Truth was, in striving to understand Kane's intentions he was mentally clutching at straws. The only certainty was that the man had to be stopped.

Violet Goodwine estimated Kane had a fifteen-minute start. There was a chance they'd gain some on him, be more like ten minutes behind when they crossed the river at the ford. But their horses were still weary from the fast crossing of the Big Bend Desert, and they were up against mounts fresh from time spent grazing on the lush banks of the Rio Grande.

The rough track took them along the river and barely touched Nathan's Ford's western edge. A few single-storey private dwellings to their left were scarcely sheltered from the sun by parched trees; washing flapped on lines. The backs of the business premises flanking the north side of the town's main street loomed ahead of them. Then they were on to the hard dirt at the western end of the road and swinging down the slope that took them into the river.

The ford was shallow, the riverbed mud and gravel. They splashed across, the bright sun painting dazzling rainbows in the spray kicked up by the flashing hoofs. As they pushed up the far bank and into Mexico, a loaded wagon pulled by a team of mules was being eased down towards the water by the muleskinner.

Lukus pulled alongside.

'Two riders,' he called, 'moving fast, heading south. D'you see them?'

The 'skinner was burly, bald, unshaven.

He spat tobacco in a yellow stream, flicked his whip at the river.

'What? Not south,' he shouted.

'You saying they crossed here? Back into Texas?'

'Rode into town,' he shouted, gesturing, then stood up and began working hard on the brake as the heavy wagon rolled forward and began pushing the team.

Lukus pulled away as dust from the big wheels billowed in thick clouds. He coughed as Travis joined him, and shook his head in disgust.

'You were right, I got it wrong,' he said. 'John Fallon Kane's gone after the money.'

19

They overtook the big wagon in midstream, splashing past the labouring team of mules and up into Nathan's Ford's main street. Travis caught up with Lukus, leaned out from his horse to grab the other man's arm.

'Frank Bellard's there, in a chair outside the jail. If he sees you . . . '

'Nothing we can do but brazen it out,' Lukus said. 'Ride by, give him a wave.'

'That's not going to work.'

'Then leave me to it. Go talk to Frank.'

'What about Fallon? He's a tough nut to crack.'

'But he's got Kris, he'll use him, and that makes it my problem.'

Travis peeled away, turned towards the jail. Lukus put spurs to the big roan and rode up the middle of the street at a flat-out gallop. He heard Bellard yell, glanced back briefly to see him on his feet and gesticulating as Will Travis swung down from his horse.

Then he was through the town, past the Wayfarer saloon, the livery barn, past the hotel where Lil Lavender had briefly stayed, and out on to the trail that snaked north towards the Rheingold spread.

* * *

Lukus found John Fallon Kane in the small graveyard tucked into the woods behind the house. He was drawn there by the murmur of distant voices as he dismounted and tied the roan.

Instinct, not thought, made him leave the Winchester in its boot. The same instinct saw him check his six-gun, hitch his belt and bend to tie the holster's rawhide thongs about his right thigh. Six-guns have been known to snag on leather. If this came to a gunfight, the man struggling to draw his

Colt would be the man to die.

That done, feeling weariness as an unbearable weight after the long desert crossing and the morning's hard riding, Lukus walked a little stiffly round the house and across the yard.

The sun was drawing the scent of pine resin from Kris's pile of cut logs. The corral was empty and, along with the empty house and the space by the corral where the buckboard usually stood, gave the property an air of desolation. A feeling of intense foreboding swept over Lukus as he ran a hand along one of the corral's peeled poles and set off across the grassy slope towards the cemetery. But it was a foreboding beyond his understanding and he advanced without caution, realizing intuitively that he was needed and would not be cut down in cold blood.

When his footsteps softened on pine needles as he entered the dappled shadows under the trees, the foreboding gave way to sadness, then to an unexpected surge of determination that was dizzying in its intensity.

There were three plain wooden crosses, marking three family graves. Lukus knew that he would fight to his last breath to make sure the fourth would be a long time coming.

'Well, damn me, it's show time and look who's turned up.'

The gunslinger was leaning against the trunk of a tall pine. Dressed all in black he seemed to melt into the shadows. His face was pale, his eyes like glass slivers. A six-gun dangled from his hand. Even in the gloom Lukus could see that the hammer was cocked.

A short distance away Kris was up on his horse, sitting tense in the saddle. It was the first time Lukus had seen his brother since he had been taken. He was shocked by the bruises turning a yellow-purple on his face, the crooked nose from which blood still dribbled. The beaten man's wrists were tied behind his back. There was a rough hemp noose about his neck, drawn tight under his chin. The rope was taut, forcing him to strain his head back and up to avoid choking. The rope's end had been tossed across a branch, and secured.

The horse was trembling. Its ears were back, its eyes enormous. It could sense the atmosphere, sense the menace in the man leaning against the tree; somehow feel the terrible fear in the man whose weight it was bearing.

It wanted out of there. The snap of a twig, a sudden movement was all that was needed — and if the horse bolted, Kris would die kicking.

'Why here?' Lukus said, gesturing at the graves. 'You got no respect for the dead?'

'The only respect I've got is for money, and life,' Kane said. 'Mine, that is,' and his chuckle was cruel. 'These're the most convenient trees. I'm in a hurry, and all men fear hanging.'

'What do you want?'

'Your brother told me Chancer's cash was in the house. I looked. He lied.'

'You know Chancer's dead? Killed by the woman?'

Teeth gleamed in a smile. 'Is that a fact? Well, it's interesting, but of no account. Your brother lied, so now it's up to you. You tell me where that cash is lying — '

'We handed it over to the law in Nathan's Ford.'

'If that's the story you're sticking to then it ends here. Once, long ago, you killed my brother. So now I put a bullet through your black heart, the shot spooks the horse and your brother's neck gets stretched.'

It was, Lukus saw clearly, the situation in Chancer's office turned on its head. This time the lean gunslinger had the drop. Lukus had beaten him and sent a bullet slicing across his arm back in Wasteland, but even with the advantage being his, it had been a close call. He had been willing to take that chance, because it had been his life on the line. But if he went for his gun here, and failed to draw before Fallon let the hammer fall, Kris would die.

Yet if, somehow, he managed to beat the gunman to the draw, what then? A shot, any shot, would see the horse bolt from under Kris. Even the fastest of draws would leave Lukus helpless, unable to pull the trigger.

'All right,' he said, hearing the hoarseness in his voice. 'Chancer was responsible for my kid brother's death. We thought it only right the money we stole should be his.'

'Dammit!' Fallon swore softly. 'You telling me the cash is buried in that grave?'

Lukus nodded.

Fallon stepped out of the shadows. A shaft of sunlight caught his face. His eyes were ablaze with greed, but his attention was still on Lukus, on the six-gun lashed to his thigh. The gunslinger was suspicious: he'd been fooled once; was this another lie meant to buy time?

Then his glance flicked to the newest of the wooden crosses, to the mound of dark earth — and he jerked his head.

'Dig it up.'

The command was emphasized with a waggle of the cocked six-gun.

There was an old wooden toolbox in the trees. Rusty hinges squealed as Lukus lifted the lid. He took out a spade, walked over to Christian Rheingold's grave and began to dig. The work was easy. The earth was loose — it crossed Lukus's mind that it was looser than it should have been, but it was less than a week since they'd buried the money, so . . .

'Hurry it up.'

'This is my kid brother's grave,' Lukus said tightly. 'I'll take all the time I need, and damn you to hell and back, Fallon.'

Then the spade's edge scraped on wood. Lukus bent, peered into the hole. He scraped loose earth from the coffin lid, saw the white of fresh pine; flung the spade to one side and stepped back in consternation.

'It's gone. The money's not there.'

There was a moment of silence, intensified by the hot stillness under the trees. It was broken by Kris.

'Lukus,' he said.

The voice was choked. In it there was disbelief, and such a depth of despair it broke Lukus's heart. He flashed a glance at his brother, saw the panic in his eyes, opened his mouth to call, to shout reassurance . . .

Then a movement snapped his eyes back to Fallon. The man's face had hardened. His lips were drawn back in a snarl of hatred. He'd swung to face Lukus. His right arm was lifting the six-gun. To Lukus it seemed as if everything was happening in slow motion.

He thought, *I can do this, now, yes, I must do it*, and his hand flashed down, his fingers curled around the butt of his six-gun; it came smoothly out of the tied holster . . .

A shot rang out.

As if by magic, a hole appeared in the centre of John Fallon Kane's forehead.

His hat flew off. The gunman staggered backwards, twisted and fell flat on his face. The six-gun flew from his hand. When it hit the ground, the hammer snapped down on the bullet and a second shot rang out.

The horse bolted. It took off from under Kris and the bound man dropped.

As Lukus screamed, 'No, Kris, no,' he hit the end of the rope. Kris bounced like a doll on elastic. The noose snapped tight. Then Lukus reached him. He flung himself at the kicking figure, wrapped his arms around his brother's thighs, braced his legs and his weary muscles, and lifted. He held Kris high. Bore the weight.

The kicking slowed, ceased. He heard a strangled intake of breath, a choked cough, someone whispering, 'Jesus Christ, oh, Jesus Christ,' and he recognized his own, agonized voice.

Then he stood there. The sweat was streaming down his face. There was a knife in his pocket. To reach it, he had to release his brother. If he did that, Kris would begin to die. Once he had the knife in his hand he could still save Kris by cutting the rope. But Kris's feet were a long way from the ground, he was six feet tall and the rope was out of Lukus's reach.

He could run around like a madman, look for a log, something to stand on, struggle to drag the old toolbox that was half buried — but all this would take time and how long can a man live without oxygen . . . ?

With his face pressed against the coarse cloth at his brother's hip, Lukus Rheingold stood and listened to the pounding of his own heart, to his brother's laboured breathing, to the deathly silence in the woods.

To the whisper, then the thunder, of rapidly approaching hoofbeats.

★ ★ ★

It was Will Travis who cut Kris down. He'd ridden fast up the slope and come crashing into the woods on his horse, ducking under hanging branches, to take in the situation at a glance. He brought the horse in close to the hanging man, took out his pocket knife and reached up to cut through the slack rope. The two brothers collapsed in a heap, Kris on top.

Lukus rolled out from under his brother's weight. He sat up, climbed wearily to his feet, then pulled Kris up and held his arm as he wobbled, drew several shaky breaths.

Travis watched him with concern.

'You OK?'

Kris spread his hands, tried to shrug his shoulders but found it too painful. He limped away, looked down at the dead gunslinger. His hand was at his neck, and his voice was hoarse but remarkably strong when he flashed a smile at the lawyer.

'I'll live,' he said, 'thanks to you, Will.'

'It was a fine rifle shot, Will,' Lukus said. 'I was trying to work out how to down Fallon without spooking that horse. You were too far away to know exactly what was going on, but I have to say the shot that saved my life came uncomfortably close to killing Kris.'

'Even the best of lawyers can't argue against the consequences,' Will said, 'but in the circumstances I have to plead not guilty.'

'What's that supposed to mean?'

'It wasn't me. I didn't bring my rifle. I didn't fire that shot.'

20

A week later Marshal Jed Crane brought the Rheingold buckboard into Nathan's Ford with his horse following on a lead rope. He called in at Frank Bellard's jail to listen to the story of the action in the cemetery; then he went to Will Travis's office to voice some facts and conjecturing of his own.

Travis was away, talking to a client at a distant ranch. Lukus and Kris were drinking the lawyer's whiskey.

'By rights,' Crane said, 'I should take you both in. Robbery was committed, on my territory. Trouble is, the man who was robbed is dead, and the stolen money has gone God knows where.'

'It must have been taken from the grave,' Lukus said, 'during the short time me and Will were chasing up and down the riverbank. The only person who could have worked out where it was stashed was Lil Lavender. She was in the cemetery with us before we left for Wasteland. Trouble is, Lavender was locked up in your jail for murdering Blackjack Chancer.'

'Diamond Lil Malone,' Crane corrected, 'and yes, she was — and she wasn't.' He helped himself to a drink before dropping into Travis's chair and slapping his Stetson on the desk.

'I had work to do elsewhere. My deputy, Buck Aitken, is too gallant by half. That makes him a sucker for a woman's . . . fragility, shall we say? By the time you left Wasteland he'd collected unexpected bruises and she was leaving town on a stolen horse.' He grinned ruefully. 'My horse.'

'So it was her,' Kris said. 'And she'd dug that money up before Fallon put me on a horse and strung me from a tall tree.'

'Then waited on the other side of the woods,' Lukus said. 'I turned up, there was an altercation and she shot Fallon.' He frowned. 'But that doesn't make

227

sense. She could see what was going on. She must have known her shot would spook the horse, leave you hanging and me helpless.'

'I say she had it all figured out,' Crane said. 'Not at the outset, because she couldn't have known how events would unfold. But once she did know, she took advantage.'

'I still don't understand. OK, she lied, she's a gambler and the hotel story was hogwash. But she asked for my help; through me she got to Chancer.'

'Which must have pleased him no end,' Crane said wryly.

He sipped his whiskey, taking his time. 'There's something else you two should know. When Chancer got his chest all shredded by Malone's shotgun, one of his outraged croupiers came storming into my office. Told me that on that night, a month or so back when your kid brother died, this feller saw it all.

'There was a crowd around the craps table. It was Diamond Lil's turn to play, but your brother wouldn't give up the dice for her to roll. Next thing was a knife flashed, the kid was bleeding all over the craps table and Lil was out the door.'

There was a sudden silence in the office. The door was open, the sound of boots, horses trundling wagons drifted in with the dust motes that floated in the hot sunlight. Travis's chair creaked as Crane eased his weight.

'She wanted us dead, every one of us, so she'd be clear away with the money,' Kris suggested.

Crane shrugged. 'Who knows what was in her mind?'

'So where the hell is she?' Lukus said softly.

'You want my opinion?' Crane raised his crystal glass, squinted through the amber liquid at the sun. 'I'm a lawman in a town called Wasteland, but there's another, vast wasteland a river's breadth away from Nathan's Ford. Huge swathes of land beaten by the sun, gets rained on once in ten years.

'That Mexican wasteland stretches for hundreds of miles in all directions, comes up against what they know as the Rio Bravo. The convenient border. A man commits a crime here and crosses that river, he's out of reach of Texas law and can disappear without trace. Gone for good. Man, or woman.'

'I think you're wrong,' Lukus said.

'I'm open to suggestions.'

'She's got too much money now, was always driven by burning ambition. You said it yourself: when the gambling ban came into force she was out of town on some business deal. Forget Mexico. I'd say we've not heard the last of Diamond Lil Malone.'

'Even if I was a gambling man, I wouldn't risk a bet,' Crane said, rising and making for the door. 'We know what she can do with a shotgun, rifle or a gambler's derringer pistol. And if she does come back, thinking about what that hellcat's likely to be calling herself next time around could drive any decent lawman to drink.'

With a grin and a nod he slapped on his hat and crossed the plank walk to Nathan's Ford's hot, dusty main street.

We do hope that you have enjoyed reading this large print book.

Did you know that all of our titles are available for purchase?

We publish a wide range of high quality large print books including:
Romances, Mysteries, Classics
General Fiction
Non Fiction and Westerns

Special interest titles available in large print are:
The Little Oxford Dictionary
Music Book, Song Book
Hymn Book, Service Book

Also available from us courtesy of Oxford University Press:
Young Readers' Dictionary
(large print edition)
Young Readers' Thesaurus
(large print edition)

For further information or a free brochure, please contact us at:
Ulverscroft Large Print Books Ltd.,
The Green, Bradgate Road, Anstey,
Leicester, LE7 7FU, England.
Tel: (00 44) **0116 236 4325**
Fax: (00 44) **0116 234 0205**

Other titles in the
Linford Western Library:

A FINAL SHOOT-OUT

J. D. Kincaid

When Abe Fletcher is released from prison, he's anxious to reclaim his inheritance — a beautiful and flourishing ranch. At the same time, bank robbers Red Ned Davis and Hank Jolley are fleeing from justice and holed up with Jolley's cousin, Vic Morgan. After a chance encounter between Abe and Vic, the outlaws agree to help Abe regain his inheritance — for a price. However, their plans go awry due to the unexpected intervention of a seductive saloon singer, Arizona Audrey, and the famous Kentuckian gunfighter, Jack Stone . . .

SCATTERGUN SMITH

Max Gunn

When Scattergun Smith sets out after the infamous outlaw Bradley Black, his search leads him across dangerous terrain, and every fibre of his being tells him that he is travelling headfirst into the jaws of trouble. But Black has both wronged the youngster Smith and killed innocent people, and has to pay. Scattergun is determined to catch and end the life of the ruthless outlaw before Black claims fresh victims. It will take every ounce of his renowned expertise to stop him, and prove why he is called Scattergun Smith.